ALL THE ANXIOUS GIRLS ON EARTH

all the Anxious girls on earth

ZSUZSI GARTNER

PATRICK CREAN EDITIONS

an imprint of

KEY PORTER BOOKS

Canadian Cataloguing in Publication Data

Gartner, Zsuzsi
    All the anxious girls on earth

ISBN 1-55263-029-3

1. Title.

PS8563.A6747A77 1999   C813'.54   C98-932993-3
PR9199.3.G37A77 1999

THE CANADA COUNCIL | LE CONSEIL DES ARTS
FOR THE ARTS | DU CANADA
SINCE 1957 | DEPUIS 1957

The publisher gratefully acknowledges the support of the Canada Council for the Arts
and the Ontario Arts Council for its publishing program.

Canada

We acknowledge the financial support of the Government of Canada through the Book
Publishing Industry Development Program (BPIDP) for our publishing activities.

Key Porter Books Limited
70 The Esplanade
Toronto, Ontario
Canada M5E IR2

www.keyporter.com

Electronic formatting: Heidy Lawrance Associates
Design: Peter Maher

Printed and bound in Canada

99 00 01 02 6 5 4 3 2 1

*This is a work of fiction. Any resemblances to real persons, living or dead, are a figment of the reader's
own lively imagination.*

Some of these stories, in a slightly different form, have been previously published:

"How to Survive in the Bush" in *Saturday Night*; "The Tragedy of Premature Death Among
Geniuses" in *Prairie Fire*; "The Nature of Pure Evil" in *Western Living* and in *Vital Signs: New
Canadian Women Writers* (Oberon Press, 1997).

For My Mother

better a live liar than a dead hero
—Tessie Greenglass's advice to her daughter,
Ethel Rosenberg

contents

How to Survive
in the Bush

The first thing he will tell you is that all the men who graduated with him from helicopter school —and they were all men—are dead. At the age of thirty-seven he was the only one left, so he quit. Now he reconstructs vintage aircraft in a hand-built hangar the size of a three-car garage.

You will ask: "How do you live with all those ghosts?"

He will say: "Every day is Halloween."

The last thing he will tell you is that you're welcome aboard, as he folds himself into an impossibly small cockpit to test-fly a rebuilt 1941 Tiger Moth from the East Kootenays to Calgary. An impossibly long distance that far off the ground. You will search for something in his eyes but will find only cumulonimbus clouds reflected from a turbulent sky. The impossibilities will seem overwhelming and you will get into your car and drive, low to the ground in your bruise-blue Mazda, sturdy as a Tonka toy, all the way back to the coastal city.

What will be more difficult will be what comes in between. The day-to-day survival.

Make Noise: At first it will all seem funny. You'll sing, with a Hungarian accent, "DarlingIloveyoubutgiveme-ParkAvenue!" But you haven't worn high heels since high school. You loathe miniature poodles. Penthouse suites make you dizzy. The contrasts will be more a matter of belief. You believe the bush is a place to go visit, not a place to live. It's unbearably quiet at night. But love, you will think—great big, gasping, groaning, slurping, sucking, moaning, jubilantly insane love; that waltz you dirty, hold you to the ceiling, push you up against the brick wall love; that clanking, spewing, honking, cotton candy-coloured, tuba large, tom-tom patterned, choo-choo train whooshing through the tunnel love—will fill in that silence, make a wailing mess of the coniferous, deciduous night that shrinks you down, makes you small. But his kisses will fall like moths. He will wrap you in a lazy, silky cocoon. The silence will grow more intense.

You have a friend who would be happy out there. A woman who notices the thinly veined, silvery undersides of leaves and has paddled a canoe on a Northern Ontario lake within yards of a moose. She can even name that flap of skin hanging from a moose's neck. "Dewlap," she tells you, but you always forget. Face to face with a canvas of Emily Carr's thickly barked trees, her hands reach out, wanting to touch wood. You still think of landscapes as jigsaw puzzles, something to labour over in musty cabins while outside the rain conspires to turn the vegetation even larger and more ominous.

But this friend likes women and although she'd appreciate the aviator's way with wood, she would have little use for the things his hands can do once the lights go out.

It will be your cowboy boots that catch his eye. Outside Helen's Grill you'll be unlocking your bike and this man will walk by. You'll know he's there because his shadow blocks the sun.

He will say: "Nice boots."

You will tell him: "They're riding boots."

That will make him laugh, although to you it seems perfectly normal the way the notched heels fit the pedals of your sleek plum-coloured Kuwahara eighteen-speed. Giddyap.

Later, he'll make you leave them on, licking the rounds of your calves near the tops of the boots. That's when he'll tell you about helicopter school. Then he'll also tell you that if you were a real cowgirl, you would have had to take your boots off because the smell of manure has never aroused him.

The aviator will tell you about his twenty-four wooded acres. How one particular woodpecker has made its home on his land. How the stream—Doggie Creek—that runs through the property is clean enough to drink from. How it's miles from anywhere. He will say this as if it's a good thing: *miles from anywhere.* Your mouth will form the words: "It sounds so idyllic." And, one hand cupping his warm balls, you'll cast your eyes around your room, wondering what to take with you, wondering what you can do without.

Play the Country Wife: At first it will all seem like such fun. You will learn to chop wood, splitting it clean, watching it in the fireplace later with poorly concealed satisfaction. You will make your own soap, although it congeals into gritty little knobs best used for deterring silverfish. You will plant an herb garden, already dreaming of running a stem of Spanish tarragon along your neck, making you taste of licorice. He will be amused by all this.

He will say: "We do have stores around these here parts," popping your soap into his mouth, pretending it's candy.

You will say: "It's more fun when it's not so easy." For a moment, you might even believe this.

The CBC will come to the East Kootenays, having learned it's chock-full of interesting characters. Vicki Gabereau will romp through the area, interviewing a woman who breeds wallabies and a playwright whose works demand that the audience sit high up in trees. Then she will come to interview the aviator, this man who reconstructs vintage aircraft miles from anywhere. The morning she's due to arrive, he will take longer in the bathroom, shaving carefully, knowing the botched job he usually does, the blood stemmed with little pieces of tissue, just won't do. And although you know that if it wasn't for you liking clean-shaven men, he wouldn't shave at all, you decide to be nasty. "It's only radio," you'll tell him, as if he didn't know.

When Vicki arrives, breathless and larger than life, touching the well-fitted corners of the log house and exclaiming loudly, you will play the country wife. You'll make soup and serve it wearing an apron. Sighing heavily, she will tell you, "I wish I had time to make homemade soup," knowing full well she wishes no such thing.

She will say: "What do you call this?"

You will say: "Campbell's."

It's not so much that you will miss working. Designing marketing campaigns for flavoured mineral waters does have its challenges, but you will find yourself becoming more and more preoccupied with the quality of lettering on the bottles. You used to dream of writing the great urban Canadian novel. Now you try to think up visual metaphors to convey sparkling clean taste. "At least it's not hurting anyone," your father always says, happy that you're earning a living. Your brother writes poetry, which makes your father curl his lips inward until they disappear.

Celebrate: The aviator will throw you a party, decorating the airplane hangar because it's more accommodating than the house. He will winch up the Tiger Moth so it sways suspended over everyone's heads, still a skeletal frame, too fragile to be airborne. He will not have made the wings yet, so the shadow the plane casts will resemble a lace cigar.

Susannah, his ex-wife, will be there and you'll prepare yourself to hate her. You will know these things about her: the woodpecker, the one you will hear but never see, used to calmly look over her shoulder as she read on the porch; she is a qualified ranger and speed rock climber; she speaks Nepali like a Sherpa; and she knit the Cowichan sweater he's seldom seen without. But when she shows up, tiny and delicate in a brown poncho and holding a casserole of steaming lentils towards you, with wise child eyes, you will want to gather her up in the palm of your hand and tuck her under your armpit for warmth.

Later, when you've drunk too much Canadian Club, you will start calling her Lady Pinecone and the three of you will dance arm in arm under the belly of the unfinished plane. He will be pleased you get on so well and you'll feel sad that their marriage failed. This will make you want to jump up, grab tight hold of the plane's frame and just dangle there kicking your legs while the guests gasp and the Doobie Brothers *play some funky Dixieland*. Of course, he will catch you mid-leap and pretend it's part of a dance move. That night you'll hunch over the sink and cry, "How could you have left that wonderful little Lady Pinecone?" He will splash cold water on your face and tuck you in.

Write Letters: You will let your friends know it's not just desire keeping you there, but that you're reaching inside of yourself, finding inner resources you never thought you had. You've planted herbs, you'll write, and corn. What you won't tell them is that there are so many trees the plants don't receive enough light. They are stunted. Dwarves.

What you will write them are funny, ironic letters that describe you doing battle with the wilderness, as if the wilderness were a surly bank teller or a waiter who's brought your Corona without the requisite lime.

You won't write them that you often stand for long hours at the front window, squinting out beyond the hangar where ferns curl under cedars, their spores loud inside your head. The mushrooms, out there where you won't venture, moist like skin, will spread their fungal roots for miles under the ground, rumbling, forever rumbling.

To be fair, the aviator will try to be understanding. He will see the real you—the you that walks in the city with a bounce in your step, cocky, stepping out among moving vehicles, not bothering to cross at intersections; dodging cars in some mad, happy dance or yelling at drivers who cut you off on your bike. Places to go, people to see. Out of my way, hombre! The insistent hum in the air addictive music to move by. Adrenaline snaking through your body like electric light, the voltage so high in your eyes the lashes burn to the touch, vibrating until you practically lift off. In the city you are hardly earthbound.

He will say that he likes the way your nerves lie on the surface of your skin like antennae tuned into the world. But twenty-four acres choked with trees isn't a world, you will think. Your friends will write: "You are so lucky getting away from it all."

Be Creative: He will even recast the wing nuts to screw the original windscreens back onto the Tiger Moth. Watching his concentration as he carves the wooden moulds—because those kinds of wing nuts can't be bought anymore—you will decide to make something, too. You'll punch holes in all the cutlery and string it up on fishing lines stretched across a row of cedars behind the house. When the wind comes up, the clatter will be deafening. The ringing of forks and spoons and knives will rush into all the empty places inside of you. He will calmly put wax plugs in his ears and continue to carve.

He will believe in doing it all from scratch, which will lead you to believe in him. You who love instant cup o' noodles and whose idea of homemade is buying furniture from IKEA and fumbling in the screws yourself. He will fell a Sitka spruce, make lumber, and then saw the planks into strong, flexible strips. He will reinforce the frame of the small plane with this wood, and construct the wings, which will then lie folded in racks along the ceiling. What you'll like the most is the mounds of sweet-smelling sawdust all over the floor. It will make you high. You will pull him down, wanting to make love in a pile of Sitka dust, but he'll pull away.

He will say: "That stuff can kill you if you breathe in too much."

That something so soft could kill will surprise you.

You will be thrilled when he comes with you to the city for a day, your rusty synapses firing again. But when you return, all he will remember is the guy who carried his bicycle seat around so no one would steal it. He won't even lock his hangar at night. Oh, sure, you will think. Who'd want to steal a plane with no wings, anyway?

Your brother will send you a poem in the mail, the mail you pick up once a week in the nearest town. Out there, you will even miss your letter carrier, the snarly woman who uses her pregnancy as an excuse to bend your magazines in half and crumple postcards from friends in exotic places. O snarly bitch goddess, you will think, come crumple my mail all over the porch and I will humbly bend over to gather it up and then make you mint tea with real leaves. But of course, no one will come. The mail will be delivered to a postbox number thirty-two miles away.

The poem will be no ordinary poem, but a sonnet:

Wearing a stiffened dress of scaly bark,
She moves like thickened shadows through the trees
That would much rather see her naked, stark,
But then, unclothed, most likely she would freeze
Her street flesh so unused to forest air.
Nearby a creature stirs within its lair

And soon a coffee-coloured feeling spills
So slowly down her loins and finally kills
Her longing to be one with all these beasts
Of rooted wood. That she had thought the bush
Was something more than ground gone wild and lush
Was simply foolish on her part; a feast
Of folly—a thin penny dropped in haste—
A high ideal best left alone, not chased. (or "chaste"?)

What do you think?
your loving brud, the bard

The fact that he wants you to decide will trouble you. But it won't occur to you to fold the sonnet into a paper airplane and send it wafting into the trees. Lying in bed that night you will read it over and over, wondering if he's just a bad poet or if he's trying to be funny. You will dream that you, with your skin of birchbark, and Lady Pinecone are shopping for clothes at The Block, snagging runs in all those beautiful crepe de Chine dresses by Zapata while the funky salesclerks sharpen their axes behind the cappuccino counter. You will wake up wanting a long espresso and almond biscotti so badly your tongue throbs.

Listen Up: Mountains don't move you. On a clear day, you're hard-pressed to make out the shape of the North Shore Lions. Yet there are people who don't even need to look, the ones who can know a mountain with their hands. You will meet the aviator's friend, a man who's climbed St. Mary's rock face so many times he can do it blindfolded. He knows where the rock will rise to meet him. He will come to visit after a day of climbing, and over homemade beer, bitter and weak, they will talk about altitude while you sit stone-faced, wanting news of the world. They will talk about how high they can climb and how high they can fly. Later that night you will write furiously in your diary:

Altitude, altitudealtitudealtitudealtitudealtitudealti-tudealtitudealtitude, until, when a page is covered and the word blurs into attitude, you will finally understand.

Learn How to Fly: You will go out to the hangar at night where the Tiger Moth hangs slightly suspended like a wingless dragonfly. You will climb shakily into the cock-pit. Inside the skeleton of the plane you will become more aware of your own bones—less fixated on your skin and your viscera. You will peer through the windshield, considering the possibilities for flight. The wind, you will think, the wind through your hair might be a good thing.

It will be dawn when you return to bed, but he has not wakened, hasn't sensed your absence. You will lie there watching him talking in his sleep to his dead friends, all those dear boys from helicopter school whose bodies were left scattered on mountain ledges, glassy lakes and runways. And you will go lie on the floor, pressing your body to the ground.

The day he finally attaches the wings, he will offer the invitation to join him. But in your mind you are already hugging the highway and he is hugging the sky. You will drive straight to the busiest intersection in the city, get out of your car and lie down on the sidewalk. There, with the rumble of traffic in your very bones, the nerves buried below your skin will rise to the surface again, gaining altitude, shyly at first, and then like a thousand-legged centipede will begin excitedly waving to all the people rushing by.

The Tragedy of Premature Death among Geniuses

I am in the garden with Edgar the Human Cheetah when it starts to rain something awful. Big hard drops that smack the tomatoes silly and flatten the pansies. I know I shouldn't have planted pansies, they're such weak flowers, but I like their little faces.

Edgar beats me to the porch, of course. He is the Human Cheetah.

"Quick," Edgar says over cereal one morning. "Is any animal faster than a cheetah?" I am not quick to answer though, and he answers himself, his mouth full of Froot Loops swollen with milk. "A gazelle, you say? Ha! A cheetah can eat a gazelle alive." Edgar tears his paper napkin in half to demonstrate and stuffs a piece into his mouth. I'm worried he may be too smart for his age. It's one

thing being too fast, but being too smart can be dangerous. I lie awake at night worrying that he might be a
genius. He's five years old and the perfect companion
for me. If he is a genius and turns six, he will probably
leave me behind. Then I remember: This fall he goes to
school full-time and will leave me behind anyway.

Wolfgang Amadeus Mozart, composer. Died at age 35.

I buy some sheet music and leave it on the kitchen
table. Edgar ignores it. This is a big relief. I make us hot
chocolate even though it is not night yet and not cold.

Edgar's parents, my sister Marie and her husband Angus,
were smart. A few times I would visit when they had
guests over and all that talk never made much sense to
me. Even if I listened very hard it all turned into blah
blah blah blah. Once I pulled Marie into the bathroom
and shut the door behind us. She had a very strong-
smelling cigarette in her hand that gave me a sick feeling
in my stomach, but she looked pretty with all that smoke
around her face, like an angel on a calendar. "What
language are those people talking out there?" I asked
her. "English," she said. "Oh, Pearly, they're just talking
plain English."

Edgar's parents liked parties very much. On New
Year's Eve they did a terrible thing, though. They drank
too many cocktails and then got in the car and drove
into another car parked at the side of the road. At the
funeral, Edgar wore a little black bow tie and narrowed
his eyes as if he was trying hard not to cry. Later he told

me he was pretending his eyes were the periscope of a submarine and he was trying to find a target to sink.

I cried a lot at that funeral. After all, Edgar's mother was my sister. But I was happy to inherit Edgar. I don't know what it is really, but ever since he was born I've liked his little face. I used to lick it when Marie wasn't looking. I never tell Edgar I used to lick his face. He's disgusted when he sees the cat cleaning her kittens. He has made a suggestion that we cut out the cat's tongue, but I let him know this wasn't a very good idea.

I am larger than average, but not as big as those people they bury in piano cases. Edgar, though, is a thread. I tease him with the poem: "Jack Sprat could eat no fat, his wife could eat no lean..." Edgar's eyes go small. "You're not my wife," he says. And he disappears for the rest of the day.

Percy Bysshe Shelley, poet. Died at age 30.
Vincent van Gogh, painter. Died at age 37. My age!
John Keats, another poet! Died at age 26.

I don't know who these people are, but the librarian tells me they are certified geniuses. "They are in the canon," she says. I picture the geniuses fired through the air at the circus. They wear helmets, of course. They land in the net and jump up and everyone claps, glad they have not broken their necks. I ask the librarian why they died so young. "Blew their fuse, I guess," she says.

The TV people are at the door again. You would think they could telephone before they come. The woman says they did telephone but the line kept ringing busy. That could be. I was listening to the weather report around the province. The names they come up with for places—Hope, Kamloops, Ucluelet. It's much better than dial-a-joke, which many times I don't get. The reporter has the most amazing outfit on, like the scales of a fish. I ask her if I can touch it and she agrees! This makes me shy and I reach out just one finger and touch it so quickly I don't even feel anything.

"Where is the boy?" she says. "Where is the Cheetah Boy?"

I tell her he comes and goes.

"He comes and goes?" she says, nudging the camera guy, and I see a little red light go on.

I look right into the camera. "He comes and goes, talking of Michelangelo." This cracks the camera guy up, so I say it again, this time moving my hands like a movie star, like the air in front of me is water.

On the TV news later, I look fatter than I am. I won-der if they did that on purpose. After they show Edgar running, so fast he's almost a blur, they show me, as big as a house, saying the thing I said. Then two people talk to Carol, the host. I like Carol. She has cheeks like a chipmunk and smiles often. If I meet her on the street, I think I might even say hello. The man is very serious and says he doesn't understand why they let Edgar keep on living with me. The other person, an older woman, interrupts and talks about love. She has written a big book about love. Edgar says, "This is boring," and changes the channel to "The Simpsons." I can see that he gets irritated explaining the jokes to me, so I pretend I have to go to the bathroom. I sit on the toilet and cry and remember when I used to lick his little face.

The woman at the library has become curious about my interest in geniuses. "My boy might be a genius," I tell her—quietly, because it is a library—thinking now she will feel sorry for me. She snorts. "All parents want their kids to be geniuses." How can a librarian be so stupid?

"You sweat a lot," Edgar said to me today.

"Yes, I do, I do sweat a lot, Edgar."

"More than average?"

"I don't know about averages."

"I'll bet your sweat could drown a whole village of Indians."

"Edgar!"

"A town of monkeys! A country of people! The whole world gushing down a mountain, drowning in B.O. juice!"

Edgar became the Human Cheetah while my sister Marie and her husband Angus were still alive. Edgar was only four, which would make him one year younger than he is now. They were picnicking in a park and some men were throwing a Frisbee around. Edgar raced their dog for it and beat the dog every time! This was one of those wonder dogs that had been a star on television. I have even seen it. It wears a blue handkerchief around its neck and is called Decker. But I think it might be dead by now. In the dog world it would have been considered a genius.

Edgar ran faster than this dog Decker and everyone was amazed. Angus recorded this amazing thing on his home video camera and took it to a television station.

Now Edgar has a scrapbook full of Cheetah Boy stories, because he won some races against much older boys, and one picture of him pretending to be the periscope of a submarine at his parents' funeral. No one looking at the picture would realize this, though. It is one of those things you have to have explained to you.

Just before Marie and Angus died, they talked to a man who wanted Edgar to be in a detergent commercial on television. Edgar would run with a dog, not Decker, and then slide into a pile of mud. Then this mother, not Marie, but a television mother the man would pick, would wash the clothes and be surprised and happy that the detergent made these clothes all clean. I clean Edgar's clothes and I have tried that detergent and I know no detergent would get them so clean. The man called here once and told me they actually use new clothes for the "after" picture. "Then you are a big, fat liar," I told him. Edgar sat on the kitchen counter with his arm around my neck and whooped when I gave the man what for. So I said it again.

Marie and Angus are dead, and I say, "No way, José!" even though the man wants to give Edgar a lot of money. I know what happens to television stars—drugs, tattoos, sex with people you never saw before in your life. They cut off pieces of your behind and sew them somewhere else to make you better looking! They change your nose so that your relatives cannot even recognize you. I will take care of Edgar. We will stay home and drink hot chocolate and plant vegetables.

Me and Marie went to tap-dancing lessons together. This is before I started taking medicines that made me fat. I was three years older than Marie, but she had to hold onto my hand before I could cross the street. On the way home one day, Marie took my tap shoes and shook them by my ear. "Guess what's in there?" she said. "Pennies," Marie told me. "There are hundreds of millions of pennies in there dying to get out." I sat down on the sidewalk and banged one of my tap shoes as hard as I could. The heel popped off and hundreds of ants came spilling out. They crawled all over my legs and up my arms and I couldn't stop crying. Now the ants crawl on Marie and I watch television in the evenings with Edgar. Sometimes I don't think I deserve to be so happy.

The librarian says she recognizes me from the television news. I'm amazed she recognizes me, because in real life I am much smaller than on television. "You're that woman who's mentally unfit to be a legal guardian," she says. She doesn't say this meanly, I just think she's surprised to find someone from television right here in her library. After all, this is not the main library, only a small branch that I can take one bus to without transferring and getting confused. I think she tries very hard to please because she wants to be promoted. She has four genius facts ready for me when I get there.

I tell her I'm not unfit, not like that girl who put the baby in the oven, thinking it was a turkey. When the parents came home, they found the turkey upstairs in the crib still frozen, with diapers on. I threw up when I heard about that. "That's not a true story," the librarian says. "You can't possibly believe that's true. It's an urban myth. It's a story teenagers have been telling at sleepover parties for twenty years." She looks like she wants to take my shoulders and shake me.

On the news last week, Carol with the chipmunk cheeks said that a man in Surrey set his wife on fire after tying her to a chair with garden twine. The same twine I tied up my tomatoes with when they got heavy! All week, every time I watered my tomatoes, I kept thinking of that poor woman on fire on her dining-room chair. Now I am so relieved. That also must be an urban myth.

Johann Wolfgang von Goethe, poet/dramatist. Died at age 83.
Ivan Petrovich Pavlov, physiologist (?!?) Died at age 87.
Michelangelo (one name, like Cher!), artist. Died at age 89.
Mary Somerville, mathematician. Died at age 92.

Now I am amazed. All these geniuses lived to be very old. I am also surprised to find a woman genius. I didn't think there was such a thing. "She's not in the canon, you know," the librarian says. She crosses her arms on her chest to protect herself from something. Women geniuses were probably not fired from cannons because in those days they all wore skirts. *I see London! I see France!* the men would tease when they saw her underwear.

All these geniuses, all so old. I feel like the ocean is inside my belly, making gushing waves. The library looks bigger, even. Or maybe in my relief I have my eyes open very wide. There is a little boy with white hair and thick glasses reading a book with a magnifying glass. I feel sorry for him because he reads so slowly, more slowly than even me if you can imagine! I am not worried anymore about Edgar being a genius. Now I am hoping he is. One dummy in the family is enough. Ha! I ask the librarian for books about cheetahs, but she only finds two about tigers. I will have to go to the main library downtown. I will take Edgar with me and he can hold onto the bus transfers. He will hold them tight and not lose them, because I am trying to turn him into a responsible boy. Maybe downtown we will ride an escalator, something I have never done. Maybe Edgar will run up the down escalator and I will try not to cheer him on. I will pretend to get mad like a proper parent.

I am standing on the porch with Edgar the Human Cheetah, watching the rain whack everything flat in the garden. Edgar tells me he's decided to change his name.

"You can't change it to Bob," I tell him. "Anything but Bob."

"Why not?"

"It just makes me feel funny. I pictured a Bob as bald and you have such nice brown hair." I try to smooth his hair, but he is too fast for me.

"I wasn't thinking of Bob," he says. "I was thinking of changing the spelling—E-D-G-R-R-R."

I think he's trying to trick me, but then he growls and I get it. "Okey-dokey, Edgrrrrrrr!"

"Holy wow, where's all this rain coming from?" Edgrrr wants to know.

"It's God's sweat," I say.

"God must be even fatter than you."

"Maybe a whole lot fatter," I say, and I think he maybe believes me.

City of my dreams

Sooner or later, everyone in the country came to this city by the mountains and the sea. Some just to ogle, many to stay. People here liked it with something that bordered on religious fervour. They acted as if they should be heartily congratulated for where they lived, much the same way the contestants on *Jeopardy!* are applauded when they pick the Daily Double even though they haven't really done anything yet. Their enthusiasm made Lewis feel small and mean. How could she hate paradise? "It gets caught in my teeth," she told her friend Lila, "like spinach."

All around her, people did things for kicks that to Lewis seemed nothing short of death defying. Trooping into the wilderness with foil packets of dehydrated food, like astronauts, determined to ride the rapids, scale icefalls, bounce down mountain faces with their feet bound to fibreglass boards, Dr. Seuss hats on their heads. She shook her head and hung onto her coffee mug with both hands. Caffeine, that was her wild ride.

She who had looked into the face of death with its tired living-room eyes and laughed.

The little green-haired girl was back in the store, lingering over the soaps, dipping her fingers into the pots of face masks and hair creams. She had been in almost every day this week, but never bought anything.

Lewis worked in a place that looked like a cheese shop but sold soap. A cosmetic deli. She cut wedges of soaps like Guava Nun and Rabbit Cool from huge slabs with a thing very much like a cheese cutter, weighed them, wrapped them, and stuck on the little price per gram sticker the machine spit out. The face masks and creams and shampoos were scooped into little plastic tubs like coleslaw, mashed down, weighed and priced. There were also massage bars that looked and smelled like chocolate, and shampoo bars that looked and smelled like oatcakes with raisins. The customers all said the same thing (over and over)—"MMMmmm, this smells good enough to eat!"—but Lewis kept smiling. It was all stupidly expensive and the customers were mostly pleasant—clean, pleasant people with lots of money. No deranged artists threatening to set themselves on fire.

The green-haired girl dragged three fingers through the vat of apple-mint face mask and then, looking right at Lewis through a cluster of very blonde private school students in hiked-up kilts, she pulled her fingers down her right cheek and then her left. As she turned to leave the store, Lewis felt a little tribal beat in the vicinity of her heart. Something deeply carnivorous and sinewy. Something to do with meat and flames. A clue to her secret city? Or heartburn from the onion flan from Meinhardt's she'd had for lunch?

Lewis wished she'd said something. Later that night, lying in bed, it came to her, what she should have said.

"Don't smile or it'll crack."

Several months back, Lewis had had what most people would consider a great job. She was one of the programmers at the film festival the city hosted each fall and all of her friends envied her—*imagine getting paid to watch movies!* But it wasn't long before earnest student filmmakers from the city's four (four!) film schools started descending on the festival office, like infant spiders parachuting out of their pods, demanding to know why she had rejected their mini-mockumentaries or Tarantino rip-offs. At least half of their films were about people who go through a whole bunch of bad shit and then wake up to find out it's all just a dream. If only life were like that, Lewis often found herself thinking.

One guy even tried to bribe her with a descrambler. He had a little goatee and long fingernails. He snapped a *TV Times* open and shook it at her. "Look at all these channels," he said. "All these channels could be yours." She moved down the hall and he followed, flapping the TV listings at her and wailing, "My movie's only three minutes long!" Three minutes too long, Lewis thought. She tried picturing him as someone's son, the cream in some doting mother's coffee. She tried feeling sorry for him because he was already growing jowls. Too late. Her heart was forming a thin, but impenetrable crust like the one that covered the earth while it was still young and fragile and lava bubbled just below the surface. When she asked him to leave, he started crying.

Then there was the fidgety young man who showed up on his skateboard. He whooshed right through her office door, then braked abruptly. The skateboard, an orange goat painted on it with X's for eyes, shot straight up into the air. He caught it in one meaty paw and stuffed it under his armpit.

"You didn't answer my phone calls," he said. She thought the stud drilled through his tongue should have caused a slight lisp, but it didn't.

"And you are?"

"Justin."

"Justin what?" They all seemed to be named Justin.

"I made the film about the dude who goes through all this bad shit and then wakes up and finds out it was all just a dream."

Lewis sighed.

"Watch it backwards," Justin hissed, his eyes startlingly like Charles Manson's.

"What?"

"Just watch it backwards." And he was gone, wheels grinding down the corridor.

Paul is dead? Lewis thought.

"Shouldn't we get a security guard," she asked the festival director, "or a Doberman or something?"

But nothing could have prepared Lewis for the woman who showed up on her doorstep at home on that Saturday morning. She wasn't a kid, either. She was about Lewis's age, early thirties, but with this real lived-in look in her eyes. Her eyes were a living room of despair, full of mismatched furniture and candles stuck in Chianti bottles, dripping all over the place, a syringe under the wicker chair, a Ouija board on the coffee table. She held a tin can with a plastic nozzle in one hand and a Bic lighter in the other. Her neck was dishpan-hand red and streaked with sweat. Tiny neighbour kids trundled back and forth across the common area on their trikes, oblivious to what was going on, ringing their little bells feebly with inexperienced thumbs and veering into the cedar hedges. The woman stood there on the step of Lewis's co-op and threatened to douse herself with gasoline and set herself on fire if Lewis didn't program her film.

There were those students in South Korea who had set themselves on fire recently to protest unfair labour practices, and there was that Quaker who immolated himself in front of the Pentagon in a statement against the war in Vietnam. To Lewis, although they seemed insane, they were also somewhat noble. But to be willing to die for a bad, really bad, eleven-minute film in which a naked Barbie sat spinning on an old record turntable? The woman could not be serious. Besides, it wasn't even technically a film; it was shot on video. Rules, Lewis had always believed, were rules. She wouldn't be forced into compromising her aesthetics, and she wasn't about to let herself be blackmailed. But that didn't mean she couldn't be polite.

"Would you like some coffee?" Lewis asked. "I could make a fresh pot."

"Ten, nine, eight," the woman chanted, dropping to her knees on the bristly welcome mat and holding the can above her head.

Lewis hesitated, then called her bluff. "Maybe you'd prefer herbal tea?" she asked with her best hostessy smile, which she hoped wasn't twitching.

"Seven, six, five." The little kids joined in. *Ding, ding, ding.*

Lewis found herself inexplicably laughing as the woman flicked her Bic. She looked around, as if expecting someone to step from the shadows of an upstairs balcony, aim a video camera down into the courtyard and announce, "Smile, you're on—"

After all the emergency crews had come and gone, a police officer took down her name. "And your first name?" he'd said, holding his pen above his little notepad. "That is my first name," Lewis told him. Her mother had listened to a lot of Johnny Cash before she was born. As a little girl, Lewis had pretended her name was Louise. She later went through a phase at university during which, after several beers in the student pub, she'd greet strangers by standing on a chair and bellowing, "How do you *Do-is*, my name is *Lew-is!*" No one ever got it except a pudgy, down-to-earth girl named Lila from Hundred

Mile House up north and so they became friends.

The policeman had asked if she wanted to make a statement. When she didn't answer, he assured her that she had nothing to worry about, that people like this always single someone out, wanting an accomplice. "My brother-in-law was driving along Marine Drive and a guy jumped out from behind a mailbox and threw himself in front of his car," he told her. "Just like that—boom."

Then the policeman left, and the neighbours disappeared inside, and Lewis had stood alone on her steps. There were clumps of dried fire retardant on the doorjamb, on the charred welcome mat, and on the cedar hedges on both sides of the steps. It was an optimistic pink, like fibreglass insulation. Like cotton candy. She went inside and in the hall mirror she saw that there was a fleck of dried pink foam on the tip of her nose.

She had phoned Lila and got her answering machine. "I just killed somebody," Lewis said, collapsing into the corner of the couch, the spent fire extinguisher nestled in her lap like a small, cherry-red dachshund.

Lewis had a cousin who lived in the only residential building in the entire city that was truly earthquake ready. He travelled a lot as a buyer for a swimsuit import company and had found a lover in Seoul (and in Hong Kong and in Manila), so he was often away and let Lewis stay at his place whenever she wanted.

The building balanced on a fat stick, like half a popsicle, and wobbled slightly when there was high wind. It had a complex suspension system and was said to be able to withstand tremors of up to 7.8 on the Richter scale. The city lay at the very edge of a fault line and the seismologists said that it was due for "the big one" any-time now, the earth cracking painfully open, the ocean rearing up in towering sheets. They wrung their hands and prophesied death and destruction unless the government, the citizens, didn't do something, didn't build more popsicle buildings and popsicle schools and batten down the hatches. They didn't say wrath of God— they were people of science, after all—but you could see it in their eyes. More of these buildings had been planned, but it was decided they were too expensive. And, besides, those who could afford to live in them wanted things like swimming pools, and you couldn't put a swimming pool in an earthquake-ready building. Lewis did like the idea of doing endless lengths on her back while down below the city crumbled, although it was a thought best kept to herself.

She felt safe up there, bobbing in the breeze.

One of the best things about the building was the sign by the front door. Entercom, it said. Lewis would slink through the lobby to the elevator, chanting to herself, "Enter calm, enter calm, enter calm."

She was worried her cousin would move on a whim. Then she'd be banished from this earthquake-ready building with its Entercom. And she would miss it fiercely. She would miss the ten-gallon plastic kegs of water stored in all the available closets. He even had a couple stacked in the bedroom closet, behind the box containing the bench press he never used. There were emergency candles. Matches. Lots of AA-batteries and a transistor radio. Canned food. Oodles of dried pasta and fruit leather. This was the place to be if Armageddon ever threatened. A wrath-of-God-proof dwelling, with a view.

After a week or so of her cumin-smelling, cat-infested, spider plant-ridden co-op full of overly friendly Sesame Street-style neighbours, Lewis loved to slip into the expensive, scentless lobby of the Entercom building with its David Hockney exhibition poster on the wall and speed up to the seventeenth floor in the almost silent elevator, the apartment key tight in her hand. Once, she found she was gripping it so hard that it left the imprint of a fish in her palm—a fat, archetypal fish, like a third eye. She pressed her hand flat against the big living-room window and showed it the enormous, fog-shrouded tankers in the inlet. "All this could be yours," she told the fish.

Lila, who was on the housing co-op board and had helped Lewis get a subsidized unit by vouching for her character even though the rest of the board suspected she wasn't a true co-op type at heart, couldn't understand what she liked about the Entercom building. "It's so sterile," she said, standing near the big window, but not touching it. "I'd get nosebleeds living up this high. You can't even see any grass."

Lewis had brought her old boyfriend there, just once, hoping some altitude would revive her waning interest in this pleasant, sturdy man who wore good-quality T-shirts and had dropped a lacklustre freelance magazine career to manage a mutual fund. He even laughed when she said, intending to be nasty, "The Dow Jones Average, so they play '70s power rock or what?" But lying in bed with him up there, she felt her sense of calm threatened, her sacred space violated. The relationship was like a woman standing on her front steps threatening to set herself on fire—something Lewis couldn't consider seriously until it was too late. "What if I took tap-dancing lessons and got a little sailor suit?" she asked him while twisting the corner of the duvet cover until it looked like the spire of a gingerbread church in the Black Forest. Her boyfriend had turned from leafing through one of her cousin's body-building magazines and looked at Lewis. "Are you trying to tell me something?"

What she really loved was being up there by herself, ready for anything. It was the only time she didn't feel the urge to flee to that place she combed her tangled mind for while she cut and measured soap and swept the sweet-smelling flakes into shimmery mounds.

She imagined saying nonchalantly to interested strangers while dragging a tea bag—Russian Caravan, luxuriously caffeinated—back and forth in a china cup, as if dredging a river for a body, the tea spreading like a rust stain through the water, "The city of my dreams, oh, it's equal parts whimsy and rot." The interested strangers nodded their heads and murmured encouragement in faintly foreign accents.

The trouble was, Lewis had no idea where this city was. It couldn't be a place as well-worn as Paris or New

York with their centuries of ghosts. Besides, she had been to both and found them lacking. The most wonderful thing about Paris had been the multitude of public washrooms. There were ancient, subterranean ones, moist like caves, and modern, nuclear-age-looking cylinders set along the boulevards with doors that slid open when you dropped a franc into a slot. Once inside, music played—old David Bowie, "Let's Dance," a McCartney/ Jackson duet, "The Doggone Girl Is Mine" (what *were* they thinking?)—and the toilet automatically washed and dried you. But you couldn't move somewhere just for the public washrooms. And in New York she had felt needy, as if the city continually dangled baubles in her face that she couldn't have. And that was after only three days. If she lived there, she would grow frenzied with desires and most likely end up at Grand Central, aggressively shaking a Dean & Deluca paper cup with lipstick marks around the rim, yelling, "Money for baubles, not booze. Must have an Hermés handbag!" while at her elbow a Vietnam vet with one leg and a Welsh terrier in his lap whistled "The Star-Spangled Banner" while the dog yipped crossly.

What she wanted was a place to love that was hers, and hers alone. An oasis with good taxi takeout. A contemporary Xanadu.

The soap shop was always bright and cheerful. The colours were primary, the packaging minimal and ecologically sound. Just being in there made you feel like you were a better person—at least that was the effect the owners, represented by a numbered holding company somewhere in England, appeared to be gunning for. When was the last time buying soap made you feel like Mother Teresa?

Selling soap was an occupation, Lewis told herself, that was a balm to her besieged senses. She forced herself to count her blessings—small, fuzzy blessings with hard centres, like little lint-covered candies you'd find wedged between car seats—to have a job at all. Look at the little green-haired girl, who wasn't really a girl, Lewis now realized, but a very small, almost wraith-like person, maybe in her late teens or early twenties. It was obvious she didn't have a job. And what did she do? She came in and ate the oatmeal and avocado face masks when she thought Lewis wasn't looking. Spooned them into her mouth with the wooden paddles that were used to mush the stuff into containers. Lewis wondered if she'd come across her in some back alley, stiffened into a board, her insides smooth and poreless and glowing with health, while flies buzzed in and out of her algae-coloured dreadlocks. But she didn't say anything. She never looked at her kindly and said, "It'll crack if you smile."

The little green-haired person never smiled.

And Lewis, who certainly wasn't a girl anymore, became a girl again the moment she stepped behind the counter at the shop. "Ask the soap girl," people would say to each other. "The soap girl will know."

A handsome man came into the soap shop and leaned smiling against the counter, drumming his fingers lightly on its surface. His cufflinks clinked against the chrome trim, tiny garnets flashing in the light. "Do you have any asiago?" Lewis laughed, and then wondered why she was laughing at the uninspired jokes of self-consciously handsome men who wore cufflinks.

What was happening to her? What had happened to her brain? It was as if she was here, while her brain was back at home soaking in a bucket of ammonia-based solution. It was this city, she decided, this city with its aggressive mellowness like chicory coffee. Too many people told her to relax when they were going off the rails themselves. Cyclists clashed with drivers, and although she had once seen a guy jump from his Isuzu Trooper in front of the Pocky Store on Cambie hefting something that might have been a crowbar, it was the bicycle people who were generally nastier. Coming out of the liquor store by the IGA on Broadway the week before, she had watched a long, lean cyclist with bulging calves and an exhaust mask across his face righteously shaking a fist at the sky. "It's assholes like you who are ruining the planet," he yelled at no one in particular as cars tried to nose around him and out of the parking lot.

In the city of her dreams, only small children rode bicycles.

In the city of her dreams, soap made you clean but not holy.

It had been a strange spring. People both grumbled about it and made jokes, but underneath it all was a distinct layer of worry. The media speculated about the

causes: global warming, el Niño, the next ice age, weather patterns manipulated by the Russians (postulated by
those who weren't yet aware the Cold War had ended
and the only Commie Pinkos to be found were the vodka
and beet juice martinis at an after-hours club called
Gouzenko's in Yaletown), cattle hormones, keloid earth,
growth fatigue, mutant minerals, a Coca-Cola/Nike/
Disney™ conspiracy, wormholes in space, every expert
—right-wing, left-wing, or just regular-wing nut—had a
theory. Lewis found it interesting that no one wanted to
admit that it was just plain weird and they didn't have
a clue what was going on. They wanted someone or
something to blame.

Crocuses usually thrust themselves out of the cold
ground in late January, while the rest of the country was
still covered in snow. Magnolia blossoms, thick and
fleshy, and cherry blossoms, frilly, pungent, were not
uncommon in February, but here it was May already,
and the only glorious things sprang from the cracks in
the sidewalks and in empty lots full of ground glass and
tired earth. Purple-headed thistle, wild dill, six feet tall,
bolting, and dandelions ran rampant through the crabgrass. Nothing wanted to grow in the fertilized, loam-
rich, well-tended public and private gardens. Not even
weeds.

And the squirrels. Everyone agreed that there were
more of them than usual. They zigzagged back and forth
across the streets in a frenzy, peanuts (Lewis had no idea
where they got all those peanuts) clamped in their little
jaws. Someone used the word *infestation* and suddenly

that's what it was. The trees rustled with squabbling squirrels and dried squirrel shit rattled down the rooftops and clogged the eavestroughs. A child in her co-op had been attacked. A red squirrel ran right up the front of his body, leaving mean claw marks, and snatched a granola bar out of his hand as he was about to put it into his mouth. The parents' council was divided between teaching their children survival skills for the urban wilderness or just poisoning the buggers. Tempers flared.

The beaches seemed dirtier, too. E-coli counts rose and people went into the water at their own risk. A swimmer who ignored the warnings had created a wave of near hysteria that lasted almost two weeks after she came out of the water at Spanish Banks with a lesion on her stomach that resembled Salman Rushdie's profile. The fact that this had happened on Valentine's Day, on the eighth anniversary of the *fatwa*, was hard to overlook. No one asked, why would anyone go swimming in the ocean in February? People did that kind of thing here. People had the right.

Of course the cyclists blamed the drivers and the drivers blamed the government.

No one noticed the clean-shaven man wrapped in a sheet who stood in the middle of the Burrard Street Bridge, day after day, with a sign that read: *deserts & wastelands will become fertile and beautiful.*

And, every day, during that week in mid-May, Lewis continued to watch the little green-haired girl feed at the colourful vats in the soap store, mechanically trowelling the stuff in as if she was filling a very large, growing crack in the walls of San Simeon.

Lewis picked at crabgrass while the local historian made his speech, Lila beaming beside him in front of the dilapidated house. Lila had a heart like a monster truck—a V-8 engine that roared and seldom needed retooling, huge wheels that could drive over anything, fat pistons pumping for victory, a gas tank of biblical proportions, and was rust-proof to boot. Compared to Lila's, Lewis's heart was like something that had only been driven by a little old member of the Christian right in Kelowna on Sundays.

Lila spent much of her time saving things. Murrelets, forests, even lives. She volunteered one night a week for the Suicide Hotline, talking people out of their valleys of despair, telling them they could beat the bastards, whoever the bastards were—those ninjas of the heart who struck swiftly in the dark, or battalions of voices telling the person she was a worthless shit. Of course it was all anonymous and Lila never knew if she had really done any good. Lewis thought not knowing would drive her crazy. But Lila just shrugged her shoulders and said, "Well, you just gotta try."

Lila didn't understand earthquake proof, though. The things she loved were sprawling and messy and about to fall apart. Like this old house. The front porch sagged, all the paint had long ago flaked off, and a section of the roof was missing. It had been brought to its knees but was still grinning, its charred filigree trim like teeth spread wide.

Children trailing black balloons ran around screaming, mouths smeared with black icing from Lila's enormous coffin cake. She had organized this Black Birthday
Party to protest the fact that the city was hedging on its
promise to declare the eighty-year-old house a heritage
property. Without that designation, the owner was free to
tear it down and build yet another salmon-stucco sixplex.
There had already been evidence of squatters and two
fires had been set within the past month. The fire fight-
ers had barely arrived in time, the historian told them.

"This Edwardian lady," the historian said, the mike
popping and sound system hissing, "is one of the last
of her generation. Just as indicative of her time as an
Erickson or an Henriquez is of ours."

Now Lila was at the microphone, gripping its stem
with emotion. "This is our past. This house is us. *Ich bin
ein* Edwardian house!!" The small crowd of about two
dozen people costumed like ghouls clapped and cheered.
The light drizzle stopped as suddenly as it had begun.
Lewis felt twitchy. She wouldn't have been surprised if
the owner pulled up in a tan Eldorado and swooped
down on them with legal firearms to assert his rights.
And really, what was his crime? That he failed to see the
value of the past? Maybe he was onto something.

The protesters looked like older, more jovial versions
of the Marilyn Manson fans who accidently heaved in
the huge plate-glass window at A&B Sound the other
night while trying to get a glimpse of their idol. Lewis had
watched them on the news and thought they looked
weirdly cowed as they were dispersed down Seymour

Street by the police, as if really shaken by the unexpected violence of their numbers. After all, these weren't hockey fans out for blood, bladders bursting with Molson's, but chubby suburban teenagers who just wanted the new Antichrist to autograph their freshly shaved heads with a black Sharpie. But watching them, Lewis thought she could understand their rumbling hunger for something authentic, something beyond garage bands, 7-Eleven parking lots and a disembodied future. "Excuse, excuse me," one white-faced, black-lipped, elaborately pierced young woman had said, elbowing her way through the crowd towards a TV camera. "Excuse me, but can I say something? To all you people who have recently jumped on the Marilyn Manson bandwagon"—she paused dramatically —"I just want to say: Go back to your lives of conformity."

She looked like someone who wrote intense graffiti on toilet stall doors. She looked like someone who might one day try to set herself on fire.

Behind her wavered a sea of young people, all white-faced, black-lipped and elaborately pierced.

"This cake is so good!" A middle-aged woman in black sweatpants, black flip-flops and black toenail polish beside Lewis licked her fingers with gusto and then stuck her tongue out. "Is my tongue blue?"

It was. And so were her teeth, which still had bits of cake stuck between them and something orange as well that the woman must have eaten earlier.

"Let me see yours." The woman was one of those aggressively sociable types that often showed up at Lila's causes. The kind that bullied people into participating.

"Come on, open up." Lewis opened her mouth and stuck out her tongue, but only because she was afraid the woman would actually try to pry it open with a saliva-coated finger if she didn't play along.

"Yours is blue, too!" The woman seemed genuinely delighted. Now they were sisters. Now they were of a tribe. All around them, people were sticking their tongues out at each other, blue tongues glistening in the sudden sunshine, and laughing loosely. What would be appropriate now, Lewis thought, would be to feel a surge of love for all these playful, well-meaning people. People who believed in saving things. Or at least in attending lawn parties with total strangers.

Lila appeared at her side and squeezed her shoulder. "I'm so glad you could come." She made two little fists and danced around, jabbing at the air. "I think we're really going to do it this time. I think we're really going to beat the bastards."

Unlike Lila, Lewis didn't think you ever could really beat the bastards. You just got a chance to do some fancy footwork, get in a few punches, before you got KO'd. The problem was that you never really knew who the bastards were. Mostly you just fooled yourself into thinking they were over there somewhere. But Lewis suspected they were closer to home. *Ich bin ein* Bastard. Weren't they all? A bunch of little bastards pretending everything rotten was someone else's fault.

"Come on, open up, let's see your tongue," the flip-flop woman commanded Lila.

Lewis was distracted by the flash of something green

and familiar behind a broken basement window at the side of the house, beside the loose drainpipe. She turned her head so fast her neck burned viciously. Dry heat rose in waves off her skin. She was sure that if someone looked at her now, really *looked* at her, they would see the flames rising from her collarbone and licking her right ear.

A dragonfly zipped by, bottle blue and fat. The flip-flop woman said something about it sewing her lips shut, clapping her hand over her mouth and giggling that maybe there was really something to old wives' tales. "Don't I wish," Lewis thought, looking right at her. She didn't realize she'd said it out loud until the woman turned abruptly and stomped away, plastic sandals thwacking against her moist, pink heels, sending dandelion fluff spinning into the air.

The little green-haired girl ate slowly and with intense concentration. She had been at it since midmorning, licking each flat wooden paddle clean before moving on to the next vat. A few customers drifted through the store, lifting samples to their noses, dipping their pinkies into the face masks and creams. Raspberry Buffalo, a new one, seemed to be a particular favourite. But when they saw what the green-haired girl was doing, they made a big show of giving her a wide berth, as if her weird hunger was contagious, or that in her dreadlocked rapaciousness she might actually take a bite of their own clean, lightly perfumed flesh. They glanced to see if Lewis was looking and narrowed their eyes, inviting her censure. They wanted her to *do* something.

One older woman, with the blunt grey bangs and well-knit Cowichan sweater of a Point Grey matron—the kind of woman who could, no doubt, identify all the birds that arrived at the feeder on her back patio and had a handsome son studying geophysics at UBC, and a husband, faithful or not, who built their fireplace mantle by hand on weekends from granite they had quarried themselves *en famille* from Nelson Island, a place you could only arrive at by private boat—came up to Lewis at the counter.

"That young woman," she motioned towards the green-haired girl, "is going to make herself sick."

"You ate some." Lewis made sure she smiled as she said this, a bravado smile flush with truth. And it was true. The woman had tried the Raspberry Buffalo. She had dunked her middle finger in quickly and then popped it into her mouth. And then went off into a reverie as if the taste reminded her of something but she wasn't quite sure what. Happier times certainly.

"I *tasted* it. Even a little bit of Lysol won't kill you."

"She's hungry."

"Well, I'll go get her a sandwich. I'll get her something from the Bread Garden." She was already reaching into her canvas shoulder bag and pulling out her wallet. Lewis didn't want to argue with this woman who seemed so well-intentioned, but it struck her, as though through layers of cold air, that the green-haired girl was hers. Hers to save or not to save. She was the bird at Lewis's feeder, and this woman couldn't have her.

"She seems to prefer personal hygiene products."

"I'd like to use your phone, please. I'd like to call an ambulance." Lewis admired how matter-of-factly the woman said this. The veins in her neck didn't tighten and she didn't sound the least bit testy. There was something very Lila-like about her and Lewis felt like crawling up onto the counter and resting her flaming forehead against the woman's thick-knit bosom, which would no doubt have the sweet hand-washed smell of Woolite or Zero. This was the thing you did when there was a problem you couldn't handle. You picked up a telephone and you dialled 911. You didn't make jokes. You didn't laugh. You didn't pick up used syringes from the ground while you waited for the bus and jab them into the grub-like blue veins under your tongue.

Lewis reached for the phone and was about to push it across the counter towards the woman. Then she pictured the green-haired girl in the stainless steel bathroom of a hospital ward desperately gulping generic shampoo from a litre bottle while she showered, or gnawing on bars of soap under the thin covers of her cot while the anorexic in the next bed quietly wept in her sleep, jerking at her IV so that the stand rattled against the floor. The shadow of the little man who thought he was a vacuum cleaner passed back and forth across the doorway of the room all night as he went up and down the hallway on his hands and knees, hoovering up any small debris the cleaner might have left behind, a cellophane candy wrapper catching in his throat and crackling loudly, like the loose corrugated metal sides of the shacks at a deserted research station on the tip of the

Antarctic crackled incessantly in the wind although there was no one there to hear them.

Lewis kept her hand on the receiver. "I'll take care of it. She's my friend."

She liked the sound of that. *My little green-haired friend.* As if she had a pal from Mars.

Everyone knew that too little oxygen could be dangerous. When you were oxygen deprived your nose bled and when you reached dizzying altitudes the blood vessels in your eyes started to pop. But what about too much oxygen? Maybe at a certain point the health benefits peaked and began to tip into the red. At sea level, surrounded by so many trees, maybe they were all overdosing, Lewis thought. She felt heavier and heavier every day. She had this obscene sense of gravity.

Up in the Entercom building, though, she felt lighter, as if the air was truly thinner seventeen storeys above sea level. If she pressed herself flat against the big living-room window, naked except for a pair of boxer shorts, so flat that her breasts pancaked out like during a mammogram, so flat that her eyeballs were almost touching the glass and her breath fogged the surface in a wreath around her head, it seemed as if she was actually floating in the air over the inlet, over the Taiwanese tankers filled with Polish sailors, over the glowing heaps of slag and lime and sawdust, over the whole twinkling mess down there where everyone seemed to be trying so hard to prove they could be something if only someone else would give them a chance.

If she pressed herself flat like that, when the nine o'clock gun went off in Stanley Park she could feel the cannon shot reverberate through her body. And after that, she could sleep. In clean, white sheets, surrounded by gallons and gallons of filtered, mineralized water, the fire extinguisher on the wall in the kitchen a sentinel over her dreams, its nozzle, in shadow, like a little beak.

McSpadden Park was almost empty. Two guys in jeans and rubber boots played hockey on the cracked asphalt tennis court in the distance, having a very good time too, it seemed, throwing themselves against the wire fencing to see how far they would bounce back and hooting every time the puck tore another hole in the already tattered net or almost nailed a squirrel. Lewis sat on a bench, drilling the tips of her shoes into the dirt, waiting for Lila who wanted to show her something at the old house. Lewis watched a few dog men, as she had come to call them, circle the park picking up after their pets. They were nondescript men, neither young nor old, who could be spotted here in the early evenings, eyes to the ground, used bread bags in their hands. There seemed to be more and more of them lately. Lonely men circling the park with their plastic bags of steaming turds, their dogs romping off ahead of them and then looking back as if to say, *don't worry, I won't desert you.* Lewis tried envisioning the stories of their lives and gave up, deciding she couldn't give them the benefit of the doubt, that their lives, at best, would have the makings of an Anita Brookner novel, an exquisitely wrought—but

banal—tale of loneliness, false hopes, and inevitable fail-
ure. They wouldn't even try to dodge the sucker punch,
wouldn't see it coming.

"Lewis!"

In front of her stood Guy Gregory, the golden boy of
her film-school class. Even now, after almost ten years, he
seemed to radiate that same weird glow that had made
everyone want to throw themselves at his feet. People
carried his lighting kits, gave up their editing suites for
him, offered him free drugs, threw off their clothes. Even
when he indulged these favours, he cultivated an air of
asceticism that allowed him to hover slightly above the
fray. When he looked right at a person, beamed his light
on them, he could make them feel they were the most
important person in the world. People basked in that
glow. Then, just as abruptly, he would turn away and
they'd be left in the shade, shivering. He had always made
Lewis shiver. She shivered now, remembering that
although she had never belonged to his inner sanctum of
groupies, she had once washed his feet.

Guy Gregory was the kind of person who was always
called by both his first and last names.

"Guy Gregory," Lewis said, and then wondered what
else there was to say.

"Lewis, Lewis," he said, standing in front of her,
blocking the last remnants of the evening sun. She
noticed that she felt cold, and was surprised. Where was
the warmth? There Guy Gregory was, beaming his light
on her, and she sat on a bench in McSpadden Park shivering while a couple of morons played court hockey in

the distance and the dog men shuffled along, dejected but ever conscientious. She wished he would either sit down or leave, but he just stood there.

"So," she said, "I heard you're down in L.A. now. Doing TV."

"Yeah, well," Guy Gregory said, and then looked towards the hockey-playing hosers. He watched them for a few seconds and then sighed. "I miss that kind of thing down there."

"What kind of thing?"

"Real people."

Lewis almost snorted.

Guy Gregory looked down on her like he wanted to pat the top of her head. As if she were a Pekingese with an unfortunate face and a bandaged paw or a cripple auditioning for the chorus line of *Show Boat*. "I heard about what happened to you. Jesus Christ. Or, HeyZeus, as they say at Taco Bell."

"Yeah, well," she said, trying his studied nonchalance on for size, her rising panic a large insect in her throat, a scarab twitching.

"Could happen to anyone," Guy Gregory said. "You know, I think I slept with her once, but I really can't remember for sure."

Lewis looked hard at the ground between Guy Gregory's feet. There was a small fissure, a crack, a seam in the earth. Maybe if she wished hard enough, it would open up to swallow him whole like a python would a goat. Suck him in and spit out his bones and hooves for organic fertilizer.

He crouched down, tugging at the knees of his khakis, until they were face to face. "What did it smell like, if you don't mind me asking? All that hair on fire, that burning flesh."

Her hand swung out before she even realized what she was doing, propelled by a thick, sulfurous laugh that came from deep in her throat. A laugh edged in blue flame that should have melted the flesh right off his face. Lewis hit Guy Gregory hard in the nose with the heel of her hand, knocking him out of his crouch, and ran. She slammed into one of the dog men, wheeling him around, sending his bag of freshly gathered shit into the air. The man's chocolate Lab chased her up the street, yelping indignantly, but stopped obediently at the curb as Lewis jumped into the intersection, dodging a cyclist who was pumping hard, running a red. He shot her the finger. An aging VW microbus, dragging its back bumper, red long johns for curtains in the back windows and bumper stickers all over it (*Hemp!*—SUBVERT THE DOMINANT PARA-DIGM—*Hey, Magic Happens*), slammed on the brakes. The driver stuck his head out the window and yelled in a reedy voice, "Move to Toronto, bitch!"

Several blocks away Lewis finally stopped. She rested against a fence, wiped her hair away from her face, and saw that there was blood on her hand.

"Did you feel it?" Lila asked. Lewis lay on the bed, the telephone receiver cold against her ear, trying to figure out whose voice she was listening to. "You weren't at home or work so I figured I'd find you there."

"Lila?"

"Did you feel it?"

"What?"

"The earthquake. You didn't feel it?"

"Maybe it was the nine o'clock gun."

"It just happened this morning. You're not still in bed? It's after ten."

Lewis didn't answer. She couldn't remember how long she'd been sleeping. Days, hours, weeks. The sheets were damp. She had come straight to the Entercom building after running from the park. She showered for a long time, until the water ran like ice pellets down her back and the man downstairs cranked his Rachmaninoff No. 3—London Symphony Orchestra, André Previn conducting—up to full volume to show his displeasure, and then she crawled into bed without even towelling off, without looking out the window, without waiting for the nine o'clock gun, and plunged into a sleep of desert rest, a parched sleep during which someone tried to teach her how to milk a cactus, thrusting in a dull kitchen knife again and again. Now her tongue felt like a suede shoe, a Hush Puppy rammed to the roof of her mouth.

"It was only preshock," Lila said. "It's all over the radio. The CBC had this guy on who said there'll likely be another one. He sounded excited, like he was talking about hockey play-offs or something. They say to stay in a basement if you can. You know, sleep in a doorjamb. Oh, Lewis, I'm so worried about the old house."

"Why?" Lewis heard voices in the hallway. A nanny

collecting the children of the couple in number 1732, her usually laid-back Jamaican patois strained to a terse, urgent staccato.

"I went by yesterday, after I went to look for you at the park."

"Sorry." Lewis wondered why Lila hadn't called the flip-flop woman or one of the tribe of other jolly blue-tongued do-gooders.

"I went by and I saw that someone was living in the basement, just as I thought. If a candle tips over, you know, that's it. This, this person wouldn't come out. I saw her flatten herself against the wall when I looked in with my flashlight. I yelled through the basement window, but she wouldn't answer. I understand about squatters' rights, you know, but this house, it's so fragile. And the smell in there, it's weird. Sweet and sour. I didn't want to go in, not by myself. I don't want a confrontation. I think I'll have to call the police."

She felt Lila drifting away, like a helium balloon that slips from your hand when you're not paying attention and tumbles end over end on a breeze over rooftops, growing ever smaller.

"It's not even your house," Lewis said.

The children at the school for the deaf are the first to sense that something's happening. It's recess and they're out in the playground when they all stiffen for several seconds, even the girl hanging upside down on the monkey bars, her braids dragging in the sand. Then they start signing rapidly, little fingers fluttering, small fists smacking into palms. The birds rise up and darken the sky all over the city.

Carnivores and lacto-vegans cling to each other as tectonic plates shift and groan beneath them. Chum salmon leap through the massive cracks in the concrete at the foot of the Cambie Street Bridge, chum that haven't been seen here since the 1920s, chum the size of raccoons and grinning like gargoyles. The old polar bear, the only animal left in the zoo, left waiting there to die, scrambles for purchase as the warm slab of concrete underneath his nicotine-tipped fur buckles, and he slides into the churning moat, wailing as only polar bears can. The ocean spits deadheads, sending logs rocketing through the city like battering rams to crack open the massive walls of the new library, The Bay, GM Place, St. Paul's Hospital, splitting heads as they whistle by like heat-seeking missiles. All over the Lower Mainland, film sets collapse as the earth heaves and honey wagons shoot into the sky, their contents raining down like some stinking vengeance for a long-forgotten crime.

Piles of baby skulls, smooth as china cups, heave out of vaults below Shaughnessy mansions that once housed convents. Nudists scramble madly up the cliff face from their beach, clutching at branches and swollen arbutus roots, brambles tearing at their pubic hair and genitals, as the ocean roars behind them, a towering inferno of water swallowing pan pipes, arthritic dogs and coolers of dope and sangria. They're shocked, not because the end has come, but because it's so Old Testament when they had thought it would be man-made—

a cold, clinical apocalypse so that they could say, *We told you so.*

Suddenly, there's no cliff and they're all clutching at air.

Lewis hurries along the street, looking for the green-haired girl.

When she finds her, she knows the thing to do would be to make their way together, as quickly and calmly as possible, back to the apartment in the Entercom building.

Then the thing to do would be to lock the door and wait for the city to crumble.

Pest Control
for Dummies™

Just a flutter and then he was gone.

Daisy was mourning her brother. She had been mourning him for almost a month now, ever since her mother had told her he'd died. Her mother couldn't understand what the *fuss* was about. She was sure she'd told Daisy ages ago, but Daisy just doesn't *listen*.

Jack sat, not without a flush of guilty pleasure, at a tiny marble-topped table outside L'Imperio, having lunch with Daisy's mother. His breaded veal sandwich, the meat covered with slick tongues of sweet, roasted red pepper, was so good he tried hard not to stuff it all into his mouth at once in case he started to choke. Irene actually cut each of her agnolotti in half with a knife and fork and paused between bites to make another point. For fun, or effect, Jack wasn't sure, Irene always called him Jacques. Although, the way she pronounced it, it sounded like "shock" and made him feel like a live wire quivering from an exposed light socket, or a wet finger on a car battery, his hair up the back of his neck singed from wild brush fire. Alive and dangerous—shiv clamped between his teeth, ready for combat—that's how Jack felt around Irene. She'd had a mastectomy last year and, since then, Jack frequently found his eyes travelling across her boyish body, trying to picture the exact angle of the scar and finding the thought of running his tongue along the seam disturbingly sexy. *Ohmegawd, your own girlfriend's own mother!* the little anal Jack in Jack's head said, as if everyone didn't have wayward thoughts. As if everyone didn't think one thing and then do altogether another. As if the whole of civilization wasn't precariously balanced on a funeral pyre of lies.

"Shock," Irene said, laying down her fork and knife like a crucifix across her plate, "I think you should tell Daisy that if he had lived, I wouldn't have had her ten months later. I wasn't ever crazy about babies. One was, is, enough."

"I couldn't tell her that."

"*Imply* it. Emphasize the *implications*."

Irene didn't even bother with a prosthesis, and yet, unless you knew, you couldn't tell. Daisy, on the other hand, Daisy would look lopsided.

"I think she's mourning what he might have been." Jack found it strange to be solemnly repeating Daisy's own words. They were like alien food in his mouth, lightly braised monkey brains. He felt brave—an anthropologist in the field who's determined to adhere to some throwback tribe's incomprehensible rites. Like the indomitable Shirley MacLaine drinking ox blood in Africa, eyes impishly twinkling, gag reflex in admirable check. He holds a small metal shovel with serrated edges and cracks down hard on the monkey's skull as the elder tribesmen clap him on the back. His interpreter tells him he's the first white man to be so daring. The monkey's grey matter squishes into the spaces between his teeth and threatens to rush back out his nose.

Irene snorted. "He would have been chunky and insecure like Daisy. And, unlike Daisy, to give her credit, he'd still be living at home with me because mamas' boys are like that and I would certainly have had the bad luck to raise a mama's boy. Shock, puppet, don't act so nonplussed, I'm just being *realistic*."

That morning Daisy had stood looking out the living-room window, griping about a couple of four-wheel drives with frat-house bumper stickers parked facing the wrong way up the street. "There's no reason for it, there's lots of room on the other side," she had said. "Those assholes just do it to be annoying." Then her shoulders started shaking and she pressed her forehead to the glass and sobbed, her tears making crooked tracks down the dusty pane before settling on the even dustier windowsill. Jack, sitting there behind her cross-legged on the old kilim rug, gently stretching his groin which he'd pulled trying to hacky-sack with some guys ten years younger, had joked, "Do you want me to go out there and beat them up?" That had only made her cry harder. He just sat there not knowing what to do. Not knowing how much more of this he could take. So when Daisy pulled herself together and left for work, wobbling towards Bloor on her old Fred MacMurray bicycle, blue plastic milkcrate full of press kits bungee-corded to the back fender, artificially black corkscrew curls bouncing in her wake like rogue bedsprings, he called Irene to tell her he was worried about her daughter, who also happened to be the woman he thought he loved.

Now sitting here discussing Daisy's seemingly pointless tears with her mother outside a bright, busy café made them seem less sad and more wacky. More typically Daisy. Beside them sat a couple of competitive cyclists, their Easter ham-sized quads in electric-blue Lycra splayed out from under a too small table. Their shins and calves were shaved aerodynamically smooth. What was it about speed? Jack wondered. What was it that made some people want to be fast, to be first? Jack could smell the men's sweat as they sat there drinking expensive Italian mineral water, their million-dollar sweat, and the funny thing was, it didn't smell any different than his own plain tap-water sweat. It was a thought that gave him comfort as he tightened his stringy thigh muscles that fit, with room to spare, under his table. Once he started tightening, though, some reflex took over and he couldn't stop. He clenched his toes inside his roomy Keds, he clenched his abdomen, his butt muscles. He tried to keep his face relaxed.

"She feels guilty, I think," Jack said, as he clenched his sphincter. Sometimes this went on for hours as he sat at his desk, until he thought he was going to scream. It was always the same order: quads, toes, stomach, butt, ass-hole. At the end of it all he felt exhausted. He'd never told anyone, there didn't seem to be a way to tell.

"For what?!" Irene looked genuinely surprised.

"For living."

"You know, I've never felt guilty a day in my life."

"For losing the baby?"

"For *anything*. Have you?"

The fetus looks so much like some Hollywood version of an alien that Daisy wonders if she isn't hallucinating an abduction. Maybe they've already stuck a tube down her throat and up her ass and shone bright lights in her eyes and scraped away enough tissue samples to create a whole new race of Über Daisys. A Daisy chain. She laughs. Air bubbles spill out of her mouth and dance around in the warm amniotic fluid. The fetus bats at them with his little curled fists. Daisy bats one back. Soon they're enjoying a game of in utero badminton and Daisy feels so utterly peaceful tumbling around defying gravity. And besides, she's always wanted a brother.

Jack found it hard to concentrate after lunch. He was copy-editing a new Dummies™ book. *Pest Control for Dummies™*. The only good thing about this contract was that he'd become an instant expert in things he'd previously cared nothing about, giving him some-thing to talk about at parties. He now had opinions on

Chinese opera, S.A.T. scores, Frisbee golf, and furniture reupholstering.

"I'm sure the plural is silverfish and not silverfishes," he told the author, who kept calling up and trying to engage Jack in long literary conversations as if he were Thomas Wolfe to Jack's Maxwell Perkins. This was a man who got excited about the fact that crumbled bay leaves scattered along a windowsill will deter ants. He jocularly called Jack "Grammar Boy," but with an increasing edge to his voice over the past few days. The man was, by trade, an organic exterminator. But, as he'd told Jack, he once had a poem published in *Fiddlehead*, a literary magazine in the Maritimes, so he knew something about *writing*, too.

"But doesn't silverfishes just sound so much better?" the exterminator/poet asked.

"Well, it rhymes with delicious," Jack said. "Maybe you could include cooking tips. That'd make you the Martha Stewart of insects and vermin."

"Are you mocking me?" The man sounded as if he was drawing himself up to full height on the other end of the telephone line, getting ready to rumble.

"Chocolate-covered grasshoppers, an excellent source of protein," Jack said. "Rats on a stick—with your eyes closed, I'm told it tastes just like chicken."

The exterminator hung up.

Jack clenched his thighs. On his desk, an ant was rolling around with a crumb as if working out on an exercise ball. It looked stupidly heroic. Jack clenched his toes in their threadbare Work Warehouse socks. He wondered how the ant would get the crumb ball off the desk and onto the floor and out to its anthill without killing itself. He clenched his stomach. He clenched his butt. He clenched his sphincter. He brought his fist down on the ant and crumb ball and then wondered why he'd done that.

If she doesn't look directly at him, doesn't dwell on his unsettling translucence, Daisy finds talking to the fetus easy. The first encounter had been strange and utterly magical, much the same as she'd always imagined love at first sight—that unbearable tingle of reverse déjà vu that can have you frolicking giddily through familiar streets as if you've never seen them before in your life, falling into fountains with your clothes on and not caring if anyone thought you were crazy. Laughing so hard you almost peed yourself. Except with the fetus it was a different kind of love, of course. He *was* her brother.

She's becoming used to the fetus's burbly voice. He's been teaching her to relax, to bob lightly in the fluid without tensing her muscles. Sort of like drown-proofing. He's lecturing her about living in the moment, going with the flow. Daisy is surprised at how much the fetus knows.

"I watch, I listen," the fetus says. "It's not like I have much of anything else to do." He indicates the twisted cord that tethers him to their mother's placenta and shrugs.

Daisy explores the coral reef of their mother's womb.

Skin polyps undulate like sea anemone, membrane tender and swollen like fire sponge. A triggerfish swims by.

And there is her brother, reef urchin. Heart urchin. Sea biscuit. And it's all Daisy can do not to gobble him up.

Jack looked at the photograph of the West Coast banana slug, thinking it must have been enlarged for effect. In small print, under the photo, it read: *Actual Size.* "Bullshit," Jack said. The thing was almost the size of his own prick. He found it difficult to read the description of how to keep the slugs from destroying basil and lettuce and other leafy greens without involuntarily cringing. Diatomaceous earth, made up of the crushed, glass-shard bodies of other bugs, sliced the slug's abdomen to shreds. Judiciously applied salt would sizzle it to pus in minutes, turning it into an open wound. Organic pest control, Jack decided, was for sadists.

Some things are hard to kill, almost impossible. Others are dead easy, even by accident. Daisy's brother had been born with the umbilical cord wrapped around his neck. Three times. Actually, he had barely been born. "Just a flutter and then he was gone," Jack heard her say over and over as she called friends across the city and across the country, wallowing in an anguish he found baffling, bathing in it as if in a lukewarm tub with unpleasant little islands of oil and hair floating on top. For almost a month she had been mooning around, crying, screaming, taking time off work. Wearing black. Which she always wore, it's true, but this seemed more deliberate. More... black. He tried reasoning with her. She had never known him. It was over thirty years ago. He'd never really even been alive. He didn't even have a name.

What Jack didn't say, couldn't say, was that if he had lived, there would have never been a Daisy. She knew that. She had to know that.

Jack has thought of leaving Daisy. Not because of this brother thing, but because he doesn't find her attractive. He finds his lack of desire baffling, because, the thing is this: he loves Daisy. Or did. Or still does. And yet.

And yet.

Jack has this thing about skinny women. His thighs prickle and his anus tingles just thinking about Daisy's mother deftly rolling up a slice of prosciutto with her long, bony, prostate-probing physician's fingers and holding it to her mouth like a cigarette. He doesn't even really like her. She seems to lack a moral core. No guilt. Who has no guilt? And yet.

A few months back he had been fascinated by the new woman next door, the way she flitted around her deck, watering her herbs, bending over to poke at something that was refusing to grow inside of an old olive oil tin. Her spine strained against her skin through her thin tank tops, an aggressive row of hard little knobs like helmeted soldiers marching off to war—to blow up bridges while lice swam in their underwear, doing all those things that men at war must do. Her shoulder blades like fighter kites. Jack could see her back deck from the kitchen window and so he spent a lot of time washing dishes, wondering what it would be like to hold someone so sharp-edged in his arms. Would she feel like a bat? Would her heart beat alarmingly close to the surface of her chest?

When it finally dawned on him that she was deliberately wasting away, he felt sickened and stupid. Now the herbs had bolted and dried into spindly skeletal shapes with spiderwebs stretched between them. The woman's mother often came over and spent her entire visits sitting in a weather-stained old easy chair on the deck, raking her fingers through her own hair as if looking for something. The woman walked stooped, a reusable Starbucks cup with its bendable straw fastened to her lips, her skin sucked to the bones, ashen around the eyes and shiny on her bare temples which were hatch-marked with veins.

Just the other day, when she shuffled by him outside the Harbord Bakery, weakly slurping at whatever life-sustaining liquid was contained in her cup, Jack had turned his head and pretended to be intently hailing a cab.

The fetus never sleeps so he doesn't know what dreaming is. Daisy tries to explain and finds herself describing how being in the womb with him has all the elements of a dream even though she knows it isn't a dream—which, she is forced to add, is often the hallmark of a dream. She confuses the fetus.

She confuses herself.

Maybe Jack didn't fully understand the concept of pest control. He generally admired insects and vermin. Unlike Jack, they never sat around doing nothing. They always seemed weirdly imbued with purpose, so intractably drawn to whatever they were drawn to, like flies to carrion.

People, on the other hand, people could be pests. Like his friend Glenn, who'd drop by all the time just to tell Jack how terribly an audition had gone and then stay for hours, drinking whatever beer was in the fridge and pulling books off the shelves at random. He would read out loud to Jack, who hated to be read out loud to, from books Jack had already read. Glenn was hoping to get a lucrative audio book gig, but Jack thought his stringy tenor would make people drive off the road.

"I just did the coolest thing," Glenn said, pushing past Jack in the tight front hall and dropping himself onto the living-room couch. "You remember Simone and Geoff? They own that hemp store on Baldwin. They had a baby last week and today they had this ceremony with the placenta."

"What? They smoked it?" If he judiciously applied salt to Glenn, would he sizzle and spit and then disappear?

Glenn smiled his patient, sensitive-New-Age-guy smile and said, "It's the only meat you can eat that you don't have to kill."

"Yikes!" Now Glenn would become the kind of person who was into homebirthing and making a casserole out of the placenta. "I hope you brushed your teeth before coming over."

If Jack ever had a kid with Daisy, he'd have to make her first promise she wouldn't be a placenta eater. He'd make her put it in writing. It was one of those things you didn't think about until it was too late. Like waking up one day and finding your underwear was all jumbled up in a hamper with someone else's. Like realizing her mother's fingers were never far from your mind. Her pale, no-nonsense mouth. *Oh, Shock.*

"How's the Daisy?" Glenn had this notion that he'd godfathered their relationship, since he'd been the one to invite Jack to Daisy's twenty-eighth birthday party at the Blue Cellar Room two years ago. Jack had known her only peripherally as one of those daffy publicist types who occupied the fringes of his circle of bitter playwrights and aspiring screenwriters and actors who worked mainly as bicycle couriers, and languid women who played guitar in otherwise all-male bands, photographed well, and wore motorcycle jackets over flowered dresses. Jack had been going out with an Edie Sedgwick look-alike named Robyn whose last boyfriend had broken her wrist and who kept encouraging Jack to singe the hairs on her arm with a lighter. "Just see how close you can get," she'd whisper dramatically, the tip of her tongue poking into his ear. She didn't do this to be funny.

Jack and Robyn had been arguing across a blue-checked tablecloth, a pyramid of empty shot glasses at their elbows, when Daisy came over and asked him to dance. "I'm the birthday girl," she'd told him when he hesitated. "I get to dance with everyone." And just because Robyn's kohl-ringed eyes suddenly looked so small and piggy and Daisy's shone generously behind her big, red-plastic frames, Jack got up to dance. "So, has your girlfriend tried the Hungarian cherry cake, or has she already eaten this year?" Daisy asked. Jack laughed. Someone kept playing "Never on a Sunday" over and over on the jukebox. Jack hadn't danced in public since junior high. And he had never necked in public. The way Jack remembers it, Daisy was wearing purple elbow-length gloves. Overtop of them, chunky Lucite rings glistened on most of her fingers. He felt feverish as he tugged gently at her thin lower lip with his teeth. They may have been on top of a table. People may have been applauding. The one thing he remembered for certain was Daisy pressing her knuckles to his neck—the rings were cool and just sharp enough to leave small dents, like teeth marks.

The bathrooms at the Blue Cellar were marked Mommies and Daddies. Robyn ended up in the Daddies room, setting toilet paper on fire with a guy who said he knew Cronenberg. And so Jack had gone home with Daisy.

"I wouldn't tell Daisy about this little snack you just had," Jack told Glenn, who had stretched himself out on the couch and was leafing through *The Dharma Bums* ("'Rucksack'—I love that word. Don't you love that word?").

"Why not?"

"She had this baby brother who died."

"Harsh. When?"

Jack looked out the window. A smiling man swaddled in about half a dozen layers of clothing rattled down the middle of the street with a shopping cart, a filing cabinet bouncing inside. Jack had seen him go by before, hauling old turntables, toaster ovens, and, once, a beanbag chair. He considered the man a kind of jinx, a black cat across his path, a contagion of some terrible sadness.

"A while ago," Jack said.

Daisy tells the fetus about Jack. She tells what she considers the definitive story, Jack in a nutshell, The Compleat Jack, the ultimate psychological profile. "When I want him to do something he doesn't want to do, he always says, 'I'm thirty-two years old,' like it means something. I'll say, 'Check the expiry date on the mayonnaise,' and he'll say, 'I'm thirty-two years old,' and start spreading it on the bread without checking the date. So I'll grab the jar to check the date and he'll grab it back and I'll grab it again, and then he'll..." Daisy notices that the fetus doesn't appear to be listening. He's wrapping the umbilical cord around his left wrist and then tugging on it as if to test for tensile strength. He must feel her watching, because he suddenly looks dead at her. His eyes are large and swampy. Bayou eyes. Daisy hears a crooked accordion, the snap of alligator teeth. "I can't really relate. I have no concept of age or time," the fetus says. Her heart splays.

At that moment Daisy's mother must have stepped outside onto a porch flooded with sunlight, because suddenly the fetus is backlit, his outline edged in orange as if he were on fire.

"Go ahead, dude, ask me something in ancient Hebrew," the guy said to Jack. He dragged another wedge of focaccia through the shallow dish of olive oil and balsamic vinegar and stuffed it into his mouth.

"How about a miracle," Jack said, holding up a glass of San Pellegrino. "How about turning some water into wine?"

The guy laughed a big, full-blooded laugh, his motivational speaker teeth glinting in the candlelight, flecks of oregano stuck to them here and there. People at the surrounding tables turned to look at them, but the guy, Daisy's new client, seemed completely unselfconscious. He was an entrepreneur from Cleveland, a whiz-kid designer of ergonomically sound computer keyboards who had self-published a book detailing his past-life experiences as Paul of Tarsus and his adventures with Jesus of Nazareth.

"Teddie is going to put me in touch with someone who'll help me find out if I used to be anyone before," Daisy said. "You should try it too, Jack." Although she was still pouchy under the eyes and her face had a shiny tear-stained look as if she'd been dumped in a tub of shellac, Daisy was all abuzz. Even her hair was alive, big curls bouncing around as she laughed, defying gravity. By the time Jack had arrived, Daisy and her client were having a big old time. The guy kept calling her dudette, which for some reason made Jack think of her as a giant chocolate-covered peanut.

"That's right, dudette," Teddie/St. Paul said, reeling off a bunch of big names from the past—Nefertiti, Josephine, Madame Curie, Amelia Earhart, Anne Frank—like he was plucking them from a Rolodex, casting for some kind of Hollywood blockbuster about great dames.

When Daisy had phoned to tell Jack they were going to Sorrento, he thought Irene must have relented after their lunch, that her mothering instinct had kicked in and she was going to help resolve this baby-brother thing, wrestle it to the mat. The only time they ever went to cloth-napkin restaurants was when Daisy felt brave enough to sit at the same table as her mother, who would eye every forkful that went into Daisy's mouth as if it contained strontium 90. He was disappointed that it wasn't Irene but an author Daisy was promoting who was taking them to dinner. But two restaurant meals in one day—Jack wasn't going to complain. Besides, this was a first. Daisy usually publicized fringe theatre plays, small poetry launches, and AIDs benefits for organizations that couldn't afford to spring for a cup of coffee, let alone platters of air-dried carpaccio.

This guy was, at least on surface evidence, raking it in. He had *people*. He had yet to appear on "Oprah," but his people were working on it. He wore a deliberately rumpled Prada suit and a diamond stud flashed in his right earlobe. He had slurped back two Hennessy XOs as if they were Kool-Aid, and then good-naturedly stubbed out a Cohiba when it was pointed out to him by the surgically enhanced redhead at the next table that city bylaws prohibited smoking in restaurants.

"If you could have been anybody, who would you have been?" the guy leaned over and asked Jack while Daisy was off in the washroom. "You're a writer, right? How about Shakespeare, dude? No, I've got it—Hemingway. Am I right or am I right?"

"You're right," Jack said. "I've always been curious about what it would be like to blow my own brains out."

That was the trouble with the reincarnated, they were always famous people in their past lives. Like that woman on the West Coast who discovered through channelling that she was Guinevere and wrote a screen-play about her life in Camelot. Why were they never just tax collectors or lepers or chambermaids? Or silverfish?

Daisy returned from the washroom and sat down even closer to the reincarnation guy. Her eyes gleamed as he described how Jesus, contrary to popular belief, actually had a terrific sense of humour. *Dry as bone.* He explained that many of the parables were highly sophis-ticated dirty jokes, well, dirty for the times, anyway, but humour doesn't travel through the centuries all that well —and he hadn't put that in his book as it would have turned off potential Christian book buyers of a New-Age bent. He was a businessman, after all, in this life, anyway.

"'If a woman have long hair, it is a glory to her: for *her* hair is given her for a covering,'" he said, reaching out and pulling down one of Daisy's curls until it reached well past her shoulders. "First Corinthians 11: 15. I wrote that. In my *first* book." He waited until Daisy laughed and then he laughed as well. Jack drank some more wine. He couldn't figure out why Daisy was suddenly in such a good mood and why she was clinging to every word this con artist uttered like some kind of mindless groupie. Those Anthony Robbins teeth alone should've been worth ten demerit points. Jack kept waiting for Daisy to kick him under the table to indicate they could start sniggering at the guy's expense.

"This morning," Daisy said, "Teddie was so good on 'Canada AM'. Valerie Pringle asked him, 'What message would Paul of Tarsus have for the Middle East today?'"

"And I said—"

Daisy jumped in, "And he said, 'Lighten up!'"

Jack clenched his thighs. Or rather, they clenched him. He drained his glass.

Daisy and her client clinked their wineglasses in a jaunty Hepburn-Tracy kind of way. Their laughter ran together like a zipper, pinching the skin between Jack's eyes.

Toes. Stomach. Buttocks.

Teddie laid a hand lightly on Daisy's bare arm. "Dud*ette*. That was one smokin' interview. I owe you."

Asshole.

The guy smiled so widely that *The Ten Commandments*, in 70mm Dolby Digital, could have been projected onto his ultra-white teeth. That would have been appropriate. Jack was convinced most people got their ideas about reincarnation from the movies. All those people who thought they had been Moses were really thinking, Wouldn't it be great to be Charlton Heston and have a toga-clad Anne Baxter admiring your pecs? Jack, if he was a reincarnation of anything, Jack would have been the anonymous, emaciated old guy stomping mud for the brick makers who collapses and is carried off while Charlton Heston takes his place in the bog. Behind them the pyramids grow large, the men and women scurrying hither and dither like ants. Nothing a little crumbled bay leaf wouldn't take care of, Jack thought, or was that salt? He found himself emptying the contents of the salt mill onto the table. He'd never paid much attention to salt before. Never realized it was so white. So *salty*. Neither Daisy nor the guy were paying attention to him.

"So, Teddie," Jack said, his brain a raft bobbing dangerously on a red sea, "did Jesus and Mary M. ever—or, whoa! You and her...?" He let his jaw drop in that vacant way Daisy always found funny, but now she only narrowed her eyes at him. The author formerly known as Paul laughed, though. *A bone-dry laugh.*

On the way home in a cab, after dropping the reincarnation guy off at the Park Plaza, Daisy whispered a date in his ear. Jack wondered if it should mean anything to him: July 14, 1964. "Bastille Day?" Jack said. "*Vive le Québec Libre?*"

Daisy leaned close, her breath a mélange of chlorophyll gum and pesto. "It's the day my brother died. And," she paused, "it's also the day Teddie was born." She sat back. "You probably think that's just a coincidence."

Then she laid her cheek against the back of the front passenger seat and just looked at Jack as the streetlights cast elongated shadows across her features like small children making shadow puppets with their hands. I want the one that looks like a rabbit with big floppy ears, Jack thought, just before closing his eyes against the crackle of the taxi's dispatch radio and Daisy's altogether too bright face.

The fetus is proving remarkably uncooperative, claiming no prior knowledge of ancient Hebrew and insisting that as far as he knows "Jesus Christ" is just a curse their mother frequently uses. Daisy says, "We're going to try some word association. I'm going to say a word and you just blurt out the first thing that pops into your head." Even as they begin, the fetus is losing interest and his answers come to her as if from behind a distant pane of glass. "Light?" "Dark." "Road?" "Car." "Damascus?" "Tablecloth." Daisy can't contain her fury. She grabs him by the umbilical cord and yanks him towards her. "You're not even trying." The fetus's eyes go wide. "Go easy on me, sis, I haven't even been born yet!"

It's clear to Daisy that she doesn't scare him. Not a bit. Reef urchin, mud urchin, swamp biscuit. She could chew him up, stick her finger down her throat, and puke up the pieces. Daisy is certain her mother would like that.

Jack woke up on the couch, Ganesh, the elephant-headed Hindu god, imprinted on his face from the embroidered throw cushion wedged under his pounding head. He felt so cramped he thought he'd need help from a team of experts just to get his legs unfolded. It was morning—still dark out, but he could hear a garbage truck grinding by, cans clanking against the sidewalk.

He must have fallen asleep in the cab and then barely made it through the door. Now he was becoming the kind of guy who couldn't even make it upstairs to bed before passing out with his pants off, but his socks and shirt still on. The kind of guy whose girlfriend believed in reincarnation and was capable of leaving him for someone she thought was not only one of the apostles in a past life, but her own brother as well. At least that's what Jack thought Daisy thought.

Wouldn't that make it incest? They'd have to move to a remote hamlet in the mountains and moonlight in all sorts of odd jobs in order to feed their brood of hypnotically pale, jug-eared children. They'd have goats, and no television. Maybe a ham radio. There'd be a stack of placenta casseroles in the deep freeze for a rainy day. Maybe they'd be happy. Didn't Daisy deserve to be happy?

Daisy's laughter rang out, enveloping him warmly in a kind of nostalgia. She was already in the kitchen, making coffee. "That was great last night, wasn't it, Jack?" she called out, as if Jack wasn't scrunched into a painful shape on the couch, an elephant-headed deity etched into the skin on the left side of his face. As if everything was back to normal and they were huddled together upstairs under the duvet, each of them hesitant to be the first to break away. "He's just got so much energy," Daisy sang out, almost operatically, as she headed upstairs to the bath. She was the only person he'd ever known who took baths instead of showers, even in the morning. "So much zest for life!"

He should tell Irene, Jack thought. A mother deserved to know when her only child was in danger of going off the rails. They could have lunch again. Cocktails! Maybe she'd invite him to come by. *I know it might sound foolish,* Jack would tell her, sweating lightly under his Kevlar vest, looking furtively left, then right, *but now I'm worried about Daisy because she seems too happy.*

Jack reached for the phone on the floor beside the couch. Irene was probably still in bed, sleeping off the evening shift at Mount Sinai's emergency ward. He pictured her beside Claude, the latest in a string of youngish, exotic men she met in the emergency ward waiting room. Daisy called them her stray pets. "Notice that none of them has ever graduated from high school," Daisy once pointed out. "What does that tell you?" Claude, a drywaller from Chicoutimi, had big hard hands and short legs. He was missing half a thumb. Maybe the two of them were tangled together, still sweating from a pre-dawn grope. When Daisy's mother pulled herself away to answer the phone, their skin would separate with a rude sucking sound and she'd have to put her hand over the receiver to laugh and wave Claude away with a kiss.

"Hello?" Irene's voice was thick with sleep. Or something else. Maybe Claude was calibrating the angle of her scar with his forefinger and remaining thumb. Jack softly hung up. The phone rang almost immediately. Jack looked at it as if it was a small enraged animal. A feral cat. A rabid squirrel. It was literally quivering on the floor.

Daisy stood dripping in front of him, bathrobe open, water pooling around her feet. "Can't you answer it?"

She snatched up the receiver. "Hello? No, I didn't call you. No, Jack didn't call you. Why would he call *you?*" Daisy nudged Jack's crotch with her bare foot and silently mouthed *my mother*, twirling her index finger in circles around her ear. Jack rolled his eyes as if to concur, *Yeah, your mom, such a kook.*

"Well, maybe call display screwed up," Daisy said. "It happens."

Jack was clenching so frantically it was as if a midway carny was yelling, "Do you wanna go faster!!??" and his muscles screamed, "Yeahhh!!" while Jack white knuckled it all the way, jacket sleeve stuffed between his teeth, vomit riding up his throat.

The fetus claims to see things. He describes them to Daisy as if they were a series of snapshots. He stands on a front porch bundled up against the cold like a little astronaut, his face half in shadow. In the next one he's flat on his face in the snow and a laughing woman (their mother!) reaches for him. There's one under a Christmas tree. He holds an empty fishbowl in front of himself, his eyes distorted, lips flattened out behind the glass. He hears laughter. A green Cougar sits in the driveway. It's full of teenagers and his legs hang out the back window, his feet in sealskin boots. More laughter. There's a strip from a photo booth in a mall. Him and his girlfriend (Daisy's old best friend Lynda!) making kissy faces, putting their hands up each other's shirts. His feathered hair hiding his eyes. He wears a T-shirt with a freaked-out cat dangling from a ledge that reads, "Hang in there, baby!"

Daisy is filled with pity towards this sea creature who would steal what is hers. His desire to live has made him weak, he's laid his cards on the table, forgotten how to bluff.

He haunts her no longer. She feels supple and lively.

Daisy starts to dance as if she's a little girl skipping around a Maypole with other laughing little girls, wrapping bright white crêpe ribbon around it. Only this cord is both solid and stringy, and warm in her hand.

In the diffused light of the womb she dances with her brother one last time.

Jack was sprawled on the couch thumbing through a Bible when Daisy came home. He heard her dragging her bike up the front steps and then ding dinging the little Yogi Bear bell on the handlebars.

He'd been clenching up a storm all day, lying on the couch, ignoring the phone—including half a dozen calls from the organic exterminator wondering what was happening with his book. ("*Cucaracha!* That's cockroach in Spanish," he crowed on one message. "And I'll bet you thought it was some kind of dance.") Jack's muscles burned—from his toes to his tortured anus. If he stood up now, his whole body would start to spasm. So he just lay there, trying to look relaxed, calling out, "You're home early," as Daisy came in the door.

The Bible was a little red Gideon's that he'd taken from a Best Western in Syracuse. For research purposes. Someone who'd read through it before had made all kinds of complicated numerical calculations in the margins based on numbers found in Deuteronomy. This person was probably now hunkered down in a bunker somewhere in the Arizona desert, watching for flaming balls cartwheeling across the sky.

"Did you know that there are all these liquid and dry measures in the back of the Bible? Omers, kabs, pots, firkins," Jack said. "I guess that's in case you wanted to try the recipes."

Daisy nudged his legs over and sat down beside him. She looked serious. "There's something I want to talk about, Jack," she said.

He was prepared to tell her it was okay. He was prepared to bestow a blessing, like some kind of fairy godfather. Plink her on the shoulder with his magic wand and say, Daisy, I just want you to be happy. And if that takes flying off to Cleveland with a zesty former saint, well, fly away then, fly! *Be free! Be rich!*

"You know that scene at the end of *Lone Star* where the lovers discover that they're actually brother and sister but decide to keep doing it anyway?" Jack asked.

Daisy just tilted her head as if she was emptying water out of one ear. She was unnervingly silent.

Through the front window, through the tracks of yesterday's tear stains, Jack could see the woman from next door being carried down her walkway on a stretcher. Her mother fluttered behind the paramedics, hands vibrating around her head like a propeller just before lift-off.

Daisy took his face in her hands and started kissing him. She straddled Jack and rubbed his chest. She squeezed one of his earlobes and her tongue ticked around between his lips. Jack thought it would help if he closed his eyes. If her breasts hadn't been pressing against him, too heavy, too familiar, she could have been anyone. Daisy lifted her head. Jack opened his eyes. She was propped up by her arms on either side of his chest, smiling. He thought he'd heard her say, "I think we should have a baby."

"What?"

"I think we should have a baby," she said.

The words dripped from her mouth like stalactites. It felt, to Jack, as if whole hours passed before he could answer, the day sliding into night.

Jack expected her to eventually start crying and pounding at him with a balled up fist. But she just perched there above him, dry-eyed, waiting, and the only pounding he felt came from within, the pacing back and forth of his own heart, that drooling hyena, in the cage of his chest.

boys growing

had fallen in love by then with three dark-haired
boys fiercely loyal to their mamas and I swore I'd
never do it again. My own mama said: Never go out
with a boy prettier than yourself.

I tried to listen to her, but a noise got in the way. Sound
of my blood motoring through my veins. A dull roar.
Sometimes that.

Sometimes nothing.

A Saturday before the first day back at school, Labour
Day weekend. He filled up the tank of my car and then
asked if he should check the oil, his hair flicking in and
out of his eyes in a wind that seemed to be coming from
all directions. Hot, weasly wind. The foothills smoul-
dering. Too far away to see, wild horses ran—tails on
fire, trailing smoke. But you could smell it. The whole

city reeked of burning hair, cooked tar, sweat. Dull brown rivers of gophers, smoked from their holes, flowed across fields, small boys mowing them down with BB guns like they were on a buffalo kill. For a quarter a corpse. Small boys who didn't get to sleep that night, their nostrils thick with blood sport, their trigger fingers, their everything, twitching. Bones growing faster than their skin. You could hear it—a terrible sound, canvas sails tearing on a tall ship at sea, a border guard grinding his teeth. Boys growing. It kept me awake. Their mothers the next day would have to strip their beds and wash the sheets. Nervous mothers, wondering how babies grow up to be cowboys. Bewildered mothers, wondering how they didn't notice. One, one of them, dared press her face to the moist spot on the sheet, a faded sheet dancing with purple Barneys, and inhaled. Then her heart pinwheeled with guilt and shame filled her mouth like sand.

An elk calf came out of the scrub that Saturday at the edge of the barracks, angled across Sarcee Trail— horns bleeting, metal kissing metal, siren wail—and down the ravine, long front legs buckling, spraying scree. It ended up caught in the school field, chest ripped open against a ragged hole in the fence, tranquilizer dart in its quivering left haunch, deep in its meat. On Tuesday I would find a thread of its heart still dangling from the fence.

How do I know it was the heart? I *know.*

He filled up the tank of my car and then handed me my change. His fingernails were cut short and amazingly clean. Later, I found out he went to the bathroom after each fill-up and scrubbed until his skin was almost raw.

I counted the change slowly just to keep him there. He was new in town. He was going to Diefenbaker, my school.

"Maybe you'll be in my class."

"Yeah, maybe." He shrugged. Green fruit. Motherless child.

That evening it looked to be snowing. Ash falling from the sky.

Boy #2 once told me this, as if he thought it was funny: "My mum would carve you up with a butcher knife if she knew."

"Would she," I said, as if I couldn't care less, barely looking up from what I was doing. "Oh, would she."

One other thing my own mama said: Always aim for effervescence.

Only now does the thought occur to me: It was him thinking he could carve me up. Boys are always more dangerous in hindsight.

Boy #2, though, he was a scary one.

Jennifer Hermann. Teresa Kowalsky. Eddie Lau. I called out their names, making eye contact when necessary, ignoring the grunters, the slouchers, the dispossessed. One more year of school and they'd all be sprung on the world and there was nothing I could do about it. Sioux O'Hearn. Brittany-Jane Staples. Rajit Singh.

Then the shock of his name in my mouth. I let it

swell like a communion wafer and then pried it slowly off the roof of my mouth with my tongue.

Just outside the classroom window a thread of essential organ meat hung from a wire fence, twisting in the breeze. Gopher shit littered the field, crunching underfoot like dry dog food. Just south of the foothills, militia men were shooting the wild horses.

The Hershey-sponsored world map rolled up to the top of the blackboard with a violent snap.

"Here," he said.

I can't remember exactly when the smell of men my own age began to be invasive. Like a jar of marinated artichoke hearts, like wet metal.

Boy #1 asked: "When I get a real gig, will you come and watch me?"

He was really a very unmusical boy. His mother encouraged him, though. The kind of bottom-dwelling burbot who thought it would be fun to have a rock star for a son. The father pushed a broom somewhere and left her fantasies unfulfilled. Mothers are so often unaware of the harm they do. At least that's what I used to think.

"It's not enough to want it," I told him.

Later, I saw him sometimes out of the corner of my eye, like one of those dark spots that appear after you've been out in the sun too long—slouching down the hall with his Walkman on, tapping on the lockers. Usually alone. After Kurt Cobain died, Boy #1 wore a noose around his neck for days, his hair in blueberry Kool-Aid-streaked dreadlocks down over his sorrowful eyes.

It was all I could do not to laugh.

That strand of elk heart from the fence? I took it home. Something to rub back and forth between my fingers. Something to do while I watched the changing weather.

I always wanted them to tell me about their girlfriends. I *encouraged* them. Girls like stick insects. But instead, this is what they did. They talked about their mothers. Even him. Ghost woman who choked me in my sleep with her perfume, something he remembered came in a bottle shaped like a cat. Her fur collar still cold from outdoor air when she came into his room to kiss him goodnight. He always pretended to be asleep. He knew that it pleased her.

All that energy boys use up trying to please their mamas. Could keep space junk in permanent orbit. Could.

There is stuff up there you would not believe.

The new science teacher was nothing if not persistent. Complimented me on my hair. The kind of crimson glow strontium nitrate gives pyrotechnics, he told me. (Originally from Minnesota, like most middle-Americans he had fireworks on the brain.) Before I could admit I found this moderately interesting, I moved quickly out of his airspace.

Grown men and their sorry skins. Don't they know?

Boy #3 said: "I like these lines around your eyes." And I hadn't even noticed them myself.

He was one smooth boy. He worked in a deli part-time and little stick insects came from miles just to hang around and watch him shave pastrami. I was sitting at the corner table one afternoon when a woman came in, much too elegant for the neighbourhood. She seemed to vibrate like a hydro line. Her hair was anchor-woman perfect. She made a big show of ordering, as if she wanted a sandwich as perfect as her hair. Boy #3 listed all the options, with or without this, with or without that. After she paid, she leaned over the deli counter—she was *that* tall—and kissed him on the cheek and told him not to be late for supper.

I said: "So why didn't you introduce me?"

He rolled his eyes up into his head.

I told him they'd stay stuck like that forever.

A weekend in early October. The new boy (he, *him*) was coming around often by then. He didn't talk much. Stood on the front steps of my condo and looked out towards the mountains. This was deeply satisfying. I'd had enough of restless boys, boys jittery with the future, boys who didn't know when enough was enough. The sky was so clear that I could almost forget how the air had looked in early September. Along the windowsills, though, there was still a thin film of ash soft as mouse fur.

I just wished he wouldn't wash so often. Most of the time, he didn't smell like anything at all.

The mother, on the other hand, some nights she smoked me out of my own bed. Perfume in a cat-shaped bottle. Like hot stinking piss.

The science teacher wouldn't take no for an answer. Rang my classroom phone. Said, "$Sr(NO_3)_2$. Say, it's got a catchy beat!" One of the English teachers, the one with the limp and the pouchy smile, thought he was handsome in a second-hand, draft-dodger kind of way. "You're nuts," she said in the lunchroom. "If it were *me*." Her breath leprous with want.

She liked the way he made a poetry of science.

I could smell his wet rot. Creosote flesh. Gave me flash headaches, like being trapped in abandoned cabins while shifting timbers sweated sap. Like pressing my nose to a telephone pole. I had to stand upwind of him just to have a conversation.

Then there were the girls, the ones that leaned so close I could smell their smoky, minty breath as they explained why they couldn't stay for the test. Their thin lies whistled through my ears like razor kites. Stick insects with their arms pressed to their sides, never meeting my eyes. Outside there was an engine idling, torn vinyl seats, The Prodigy blaring from six speakers, "Smack my bitch up!" They're not the ones I had to watch out for, though. It was the huggers. The girls with naturally flushed cheeks. The Save the Planet girls with little

platinum rings glinting in their navels. Curvy girls
rampant with optimism.

Girls are growing from the minute they leave the
womb. And if it's very quiet, you can hear it. A soft, continual *swish swish swish*. Like something cloaked in taffeta
coming to get you in the night.

Boys growing. Now that can wake the dead.

He went for milk in the driving rain wearing only shorts
and my trench coat, bare feet in Nikes, umbrella held
so high above his head it did no good. I found this so
endearing I would have chewed my right leg out of a
steel trap to follow him if I had thought he wasn't coming back. On all fours, my own blood puddling off my
chin.

Hot chocolate and a thin jolt, then backgammon with
our eyes wide open, skulls flaring like jack-o'-lanterns.

I lined up all the other dark-haired boys I'd ever
loved, and shot them like ducks in an arcade.

Boy #2, scary boy, said: "I need a sister."

I called him up at home one night and his mother
answered. Just Boy #2 and her in the house. The father,
he had done something foolish and irreparable some
years ago involving his car, a garage, and a hose. Nothing
you could speak of. Boy #2, he was a hacker. Down in
the basement, tooling around on his Pentium 166.
Making decent money changing classmates' grades,
deleting infractions. The whole public school system
was going to him by then. Skin white as bleached cotton.

The mother answered with her very Swiss accent. I winced at the thought of cloth napkins folded with military precision, bed sheets pulled taut enough to bruise hips, bust skin at the bone. Cheese served mild, gutless. I recalled that she looked like an amphibian of some sort. Blood barely moving through her veins to that creaky, dark chamber of horrors, her heart. She said he was busy with his homework.

When he finally came to the phone, I said: "Hey there, it's your big sister."

The next night he put his foot through the door of my hall closet. Splinters ringed his tapioca calf. Spiny blowfish. Pulled out all the kitchen drawers and threw them against the walls. Twist-ties rained from the ceiling. Grabbed a fondue fork and pressed it to my forehead, right between my eyes.

His mother had been listening on the other line.

Then him.

We watched the news together. He was utterly addicted to newscasts, drawn to the flickering wreckage of other lives. A moth to light. His mother had been newsworthy. Leapt to her death holding onto his spina-bifida sister, fluid leaking from both their brains.

One night there was an item on a new treatment. The rest of the evening he sat picking at the threads in the carpet until it was time to go to work.

I lifted his hair out of his eyes. But he looked right on through me.

The science teacher finally wore me down. Showed me the tattoo of a formaldehyde baby on his right arm and I agreed to go to a Halloween party with him.

Boy #1 said (more than once): "My mom loves this song."

I was taking a bath. He sat on the toilet lid, torturing my old Gibson acoustic. I flicked some bubbles at him and told him to stop. He started wailing away even louder, in his seriously unmusical manner. The bottom-feeder was in the tub, darting about under my knees, tonguing the bathtub ring, swallowing my soap, egging him on. Panic grabbed me right between my ribs, grip like an angry preacher, and squeezed. I realized if I didn't do something, he would never stop, ever, he would play on in hell with his mother clapping and cheering, mouth moving like a catfish's, moustache quivering.

What happened next: I rose out of the water, a tsunami of rage, fifty feet tall, and grabbed the guitar out of his hands. I slammed it against the sink, swung it at the edge of the tub.

"Rock on," I said, handing the busted guts back to him as he started to cry.

Teaching the Elizabethans, I decided to make a small detour. The Elizabethans, as they already knew (and seemed to approve), didn't bathe very often. Even the aristocracy was rather ripe.

I told them that men and women were attracted to each other's body odour. Someone made an inspired gagging noise and they all laughed. I told them that the

Elizabethans would have considered deodorant a form of birth control. Even the dispossessed in their low-cloud formations at the back of the room found this amusing. I told them that when a noblewoman took a fancy to a gentleman, she would carefully peel an apple and place it in her armpit for a number of days until it was deemed appropriately aromatic. (She could, I didn't add, choose to place it elsewhere.) Then she would present it to her suitor.

I said: "They called this a Love Apple."

"That," buzzed an agitated stick insect, "is like so, pardon me, incredibly fucking *gross*."

The exchange student from Osaka put up his hand and asked, "Please, miss, will this be on the test?"

The whole class in the hall afterwards, lockers open, surreptitiously sniffing their pits. And him skidding into the showers, clothes still in mid-air as the water pulsed on, scrubbing until blood beaded the surface of his skin.

In his wallet there was a photograph of a beach. In the background a fat man lay on a picnic table. In the foreground sat a small boy sucking in his smile, a woman half-hugging him, half-tickling him. Plastic shovel in his hand, blocking her face. She had her mouth to his ear and was telling him he'd made the best sandcastle in the world. That he would be an architect someday and build her a room touching the sky. Sunspots burned above their heads like painful lesions.

"With an elevator?" he asked.

With an elevator. She promised him *that*.

During the night she shredded the back of my couch, the wallpaper in the hallway, thin strips fluttering above the forced-air vent.

I paced the hall, quietly cajoling, *here kitty kitty kitty*.

The afternoon before the costume party I sat in the stands, hugging my knees and watching football practice. A new student teacher sat beside me, eager, slapping her hands together against the cold. "They look like aliens," she said, "running around down there."

The ground rumbled underneath my feet. Boys growing heavier as they ran, soon to crack the crust of the earth wide open.

I casually approached the field when the practice broke up and asked him a favour. I whispered it. Told him it was for a joke. His sudden laughter shaved my heart. Moth boy. It was all I could do not to put my hand to his cheek. Then I went home to dress for the party. The lawn was already frosted over. In the distance the mountains were white.

That evening the science teacher took one look at me and said, "You're not going like that?" I wore faded blue hospital garb, white sneakers, a stethoscope around my neck, and on my face something to protect me from the nip of the night. He looked down at my doormat, scratched at something on his palm. He turned his head and stared towards the mountains. Then he said, "You do know that's a jockstrap, don't you?"

"Oh my God," I collapsed against him laughing, "OH MY GAWD! I thought it was a surgical mask."

It took him a few seconds, but he laughed too. Although not when I said I was going to wear it anyway.

At the party there was some whispering and then I heard him say loudly, so everyone could hear, just in case there was any doubt, "She thought it was a surgical mask!" I twirled around demonstrating my ignorance, pumpkin lights twinkling above my head, while formaldehyde man stayed as far away from me as he could. Apples bobbed in a bowl of spit.

The women, though. The women thought it was funny.

And all night long I was breathing deeply of his smell. I was the life of the party. Oxygenated. On.

Oh! How utterly convincing love can be. How utterly convincing!

Cat piss in a bottle. Against love like this, I thought, what small thing was that?

A Monday in November. I walked down the corridor at lunch, gnawing on my heart of elk. The floors gleamed as they did every Monday. Ammonia still clung to the air, scouring my brain pan.

He was leaning against his locker. A girl stood in front of him, not a stick insect, not a curvy glory. A solid bound-for-Oxbridge type. Field hockey calves. *A Confederacy of Dunces* clutched to her chest. She lifted his hair out of his eyes with the eraser tip of her pencil.

I moved towards them. Don't tell me I didn't know what I was doing. I said, "Hi there!"

Then I hipchecked him. Ever so playfully, but it

threw him off balance. The girl, she just stood there looking astonished.

I could have said: Close your mouth, young lady, before something flies in.

I could have said: Fish in a barrel. Formed the words with my mouth.

Measuring Death
in Column Inches

(a nine-week manual for girl rim pigs)

There are no sacred cows at 3:00 A.M. when you're measuring death in column inches. Remember, there are many rules, but only one that really counts: Rim pigs don't cry.

Week One: Even though you work with the alphabet in the dull of the night, try not to neglect your appearance. Wear inappropriate fabrics and colours to keep the element of surprise alive. Three-tone bowling shoes with mauve satin cowgirl shirt and worsted tweed trousers. Polo shirt, silk boxer shorts festooned with lyrics from the Poppy Family's greatest hits, and orange espadrilles. And, for a special treat, wear your bra on the outside of your T-shirt.

Say: Oops.

Say: Kidding!

Say (as if implying *you* have a life): I was just at the Grant Lee Buffalo gig at the Starfish Room and boy, am I tired.

Anyway you put it, your fellow rim pigs—two successfully suburban fathers and two failed fathers—will not know what you're talking about. Realize that if camaraderie is to be achieved, you've got to try a different tack.

If truth be told, none of the graveyard-shift copy editors are prime physical specimens. Dave, the slotman, sports a kind of nightly uniform, sweatpants with a Super Mario print all over them. The kind of sweats they make for oversized men that you see the steroid-enhanced guys from Gold's Gym wearing because normal clothes just won't fit. Dave's sweats ride low, giving him plumber's butt, dark hair tufting out from between his wedge. You imagine being one of his kids and living in terror of having him bend down to tie your shoelaces when he picks you up at school. Then there's Gustav, a.k.a. the Montrealer, slightly soiled and desperate. He always has a button missing off his shirt. On better nights he fastens the spot with a safety pin. On worse nights the shirt gapes open when he leans forward, exposing untended flesh.

Even the late-night reporters are pale and furtive. Little Anny on the parks board-slash-police beat only has her springy, aerobicized calves going for her. Her skin looks as if it's been left underwater too long, and her hair looks crunchy, like you could grab a fistful and just snap

it off. You will soon discover that it's all that sleeping—
or trying to sleep—during the day, with the aluminum
foil crackling against the windowpanes. Like constant
artillery fire. Earplugs give you headaches, and although
they cut out some noises, they amplify others—the gur-
gle of a drain upstairs can sound like it comes from inside
your very own chest. The thinnest wafer of light cuts
through REM sleep like a hot laser. And the dreams, in
your sealed-up room, in the hot summer air, can be fetid.

Week Two: Learn quickly that you aren't allowed to
cherry-pick. The slotman puts copy to be edited and
headlined, and photos that need cutlines into a little
two-tiered wire basket. You're supposed to take the first
thing that happens to be on top and then call it up on
screen. So during the same night you can have tacit com-
plicity in both the twice-weekly family values homily of
the in-house Pat Buchanan ("For $200: A euphemism for
homophobia."), and the heartfelt whingings of an animal
rights advocate who believes even earthworms have souls.
If there's ever any actual harm in what they espouse, you
can always haul out that delightful old chestnut: I was
only doing my job.

You and your confrères are the last line of defence
between the newsmakers and the public. Often your
concoctions—the headlines, decks and cutlines—are all
anyone will read. Pride yourself on your tallies of death
and destruction, your puns, your ability to always find a
verb that fits. Your Peanut Buster Parfaits of disaster, both
man-made and natural.

There is something about working in the dead of night, with the fluorescent lights singing unevenly in their tubes overhead, that arouses in you a primitive and playful spirit. Fish a CP wire story on unemployment rates out of the basket without leaving your seat, smartly spearing the corner with your pen of choice, a red Uni-ball. Feel a vague sense of communion with bears who can swat trout out of a mountain stream just like that. Feel clever, even though no one has noticed. Feel a twinge in your neck because you contorted it at an unruly angle in order to nab the story without having to scurry all around the rim to Dave's desk.

The ink bleeds through the hole.

A feeling of continual exhaustion will descend like a musty furniture blanket in the second week. You will be tempted to fight back.

There used to be an empty lot behind your apartment building, a lovely wreck of a lot littered with exploded chunks of concrete laced with twisted rebar, big-headed purple thistles waving in the wind, the candy wrappers caught in their prickly leaves fluttering like hideous moths, discarded syringes poised like scorpions. The kind of place you would most certainly act out your post-apocalyptic fantasies if you were still a kid. It's a reminder of how the world, your world, would look if we all just stopped being so damn careful. Now someone has decided to build a house there and the activity makes mincemeat of your sleep. It sounds as if a small army is stapling the house together, instead of using proper, old-fashioned tools like hammers. Dull thuds you might be able to take, but this feels like Gene Kelly and his cartoon mice practicing on the ceiling of your frontal lobes.

Storm over to check it out, but not before first scrubbing the stalagmites of sleep off your bottom lashes and flattening your bangs with the moistened heel of your hand so you don't look as deranged as you feel. "Why yes, ma'am," one of the guys says. "Yes, we are stapling it together." And the workmen all hold their staple guns out towards you, as if they're a firing squad and you've been convicted of stealing bread in a country with zero tolerance for bad behaviour.

Ask (in what you think is a queenly manner): "But how long will it last?"

"Oh, a good thirty years, give or take. These aren't your ordinary staples," one of the guys says.

You, of course, meant the noise.

Week Three: Accept that mistakes are made. Usually harmless ones. Say the guy is called Jack Greene in the story and Jeff Green in the cutline under the photo. Readers will pounce on this. "Lookit this," they'll say, poking at your cutline with their forks, egg dribbling down the page, congealing in a pearly strand. "Whatta buncha idiots." Well, yes, that's right, you may think, we are idiots. Idiots who know the difference between concrete and cement, between careening and careering, and CARE!

Tell your friends: "You have to have an idiot gene of some sort to do a job like this." Wait for them to disagree vehemently. Stir your coffee thoughtfully even though the cup is empty. Keep waiting. Ask for a refill. Change the topic.

The late night reporters ignore you—cut a wide swath as they walk by, sneer. It's a caste system and you're one of the untouchables. But instead of collecting garbage and burning it, you're elevating it. There's an element of fear, too, for sure. There, but for the grace of God and goodwill of the managing editor, go I. Maybe rim-pigitis is a contagious disease. Remember grade five when all the boys scribbled "Julia fleas" on the backs of their hands with coloured pens. Think about how Julia must have felt. Wonder if it screwed up her adulthood. Wonder if it's the kind of thing you'd tell your children. "I was the biggest nerd of my elementary school class. I got caught lining the inside of my desk with little balls of snot and didn't have any friends." Decide not. Most definitely not.

Anny, the dishevelled little go-getter with the Ron Zalko-cized calves bounces through your part of the newsroom, coolly averting her eyes. You shake your bag of Skittles at her, even though you hate to share the treats that help you make it through the night. "Hey, Anny, have a candy." She barely breaks stride, flapping her dead-fish hand in your direction. "Thanks. I'm on deadline." Sisterhood is no match for the latest high jinks of the Vancouver Parks Board. All that self-satisfied wrangling over whether some dumpy parkette is better served by mounting yet another statue of a WWII soldier or a metal cube representing the victims of a more contemporary ill. *Lest we forget.*

Decide *you* are a statue. Sit there frozen in position, hands poised like crabs above the keyboard, vowing to not move until someone touches you and breaks the spell. Be prepared to wait an awfully long time.

On your only night off, go to a party with your new boyfriend where you don't know a soul. Everyone there seems to be associated with films. Not movies, films. And not just any old films, but something called visual essays, which you later learn are actually just documentaries that don't make a lot of sense unless you have a doctorate in post-colonial post-feminist post-gender studies.

If someone asks you what you do, tell them you're a carpenter. Talk knowledgeably about revolutionary new advances in house construction, namely, the use of staplers. Talk about how the kickback action really builds muscles, namely, pectorals.

Tell your incredulous audience that they can go ahead and feel your pecs. Your boyfriend comes over with an achingly cool Japanese beer just as you're striking a which-way-to-the-beach? pose and asks, "Rodin's *Thinker* with menstrual cramps?"

Decide you dislike him for his inability to comprehend your shame and fatigue.

Decide you like him for his ability to mock menstrual cramps while surrounded by a post-colonial post-feminist post-gendered crowd.

Later, after many Sapporos, corner the guy who made a visual essay about Bertrand Russell and ask him to tell you what the difference is between concrete and cement. Decide that his inability to differentiate means he's not as smart as he thinks he is.

He says: "You should know. You're in construction."

Phone your mother long-distance and tell her you hate your job. "But you have a good job," she says.

Say: I sleep with aluminum foil in the windows. I feel like a turkey basting in my bed.

Say: I eat open-faced chili burgers for lunch at four A.M.

Ask (petulantly): Is this why I got a poli-sci degree?

She tells you to be thankful you have a bed and be thankful you have lunch. She reserves judgment on the poli-sci degree, because, well, let's just say she warned you. You hang up before she starts telling you about how the only time she and her sisters got oranges was when they left their shoes (with the cardboard soles) out on the porch on the eve of Saint Nicholas Day.

Across the alley, the staple-gun men are singing a cappella—"Up on the Roof," of all things. You wonder if someone has slipped Xanax into their Cheerios, or Atavan into their thermoses. You wish a talent scout would come by and spirit them away in a long, tacky white limo with a soft-drink logo on the side. They're young, agile. They're Canadian boys and probably already know how to skate, so they could join the Ice Capades doing some sort of Village People redux act. And why not? Just why the heck not? Stamp your little foot for

effect. Dust bunnies rise from the parquet floor in a fury
—rabid, grey, feral, gathering courage and growing in
number through your neglect. They trust in Nietzsche:
Those who do not destroy us, make us stronger.

Although, if you were to be perfectly honest, all the
Nietzsche you know could be gleaned from the opening
credits of *Conan the Barbarian*.

Week Four: Make an effort to get to know your fellow
rim pigs, after all, they're the only ones who'll talk to you
instead of at you besides the donut-cart woman. Decide
Dave the slotman's not so bad. He's tacked magazine
photos of Susan Sarandon all over the pillar beside his
desk along with a crayon drawing by his daughter Kristal
of what looks like a Sikh temple, but could be a birdcage.
It lends him a hint of complexity, this attraction to an
actress of a certain age. After all, it could have been
Pamela Anderson Lee. You find something reassuring
about Dave—his comfortable slovenliness, the way he
whistles theme songs from kiddie cartoons as he dum-
mies up the pages, the way his wife makes sure that at
least his socks match.

Gustav the Montrealer, on the other hand, has the
look of an unloved man. It's not just the missing button,
it's his needy air. He used to work as a reporter at *Le
Devoir*, or so he tells you, and he never lets a night go by
without reminding everyone that he's a *real* journalist and
this rim-pig thing is only a temporary gig. He confides in
you one night, thinking you can relate. To sensitive men.
Because you're a gal. He tells you he left a son behind out

east after his wife kicked him out. He spends a good part of his time sending E-mail messages to his son, who's only five but can evidently read at grade six level—in English *and* French. He tells you he wants to pitch a column to the features editor on contemporary men's issues.

He says (*sotto voce*): "There's a whole segment of the population that's not being served in the popular press. You know, the father thing. The pain thing. The anger thing."

Say (in French): "You mean huffing and puffing and drumming and stuff, reclaiming the maligned little beast —sorry, little *boy*—within?"

He looks quizzical and then laughs a fake jolly-hearted laugh and touches your forearm with the tips of two fingers, showing he knows his Dale Carnegie, indicating he thinks you've said something terribly funny. You don't know which is worse. That you've mocked him, or that you've discovered—*confirmed*—that he doesn't understand French, or that his fingers, you've just noticed, have been chewed until they've bled, the hangnails peeled off, leaving thin scabby strips. They're the fingers of the nervous little boy you and your friends shoved into the older girls' bathroom during one recess at Sacred Heart, alone with the Kotex machine, while you piled your squealing bodies up against the door so he couldn't get out even though he pushed and pushed until his small heart was bursting. The boy, Eugene, ended up crawling out the window and had to be rescued from the fire escape by one of the nuns. When Sister Scholastica reached the bottom rung, she sat down and slung him across her knee and started to spank him. The crackle of plastic was shocking, even to you. But that didn't stop you, eyes wide, from excitedly whispering, "Eugene still wears diapers." There was no need, of course, to whisper: *Pass it on.*

The Montrealer, as if he can see into your rusted-out carbody of a Catholic soul, avoids talking directly to you from this point on. Out of the corner of your eye, you'll be aware that his hands, on occasion, tremble.

You fare better with the Matador. The Matador has a trait you must admit you envy. He has this incredible posture. In this nocturnal universe of slouching men, he stands out, ramrod straight even under duress, like George C. Scott playing Patton. He has settled into the numbing delirium of the job with a Zen-like aplomb. Nothing seems to faze him, or move him. He is the perfect rim pig, smartly robotic, emotionless as a Vulcan, except for the deep pleasure he gets from hearing about stupid deaths. You only have to

Say: Hungarian woman falls in barrel of cabbage juice and drowns,

Say: Kansas man punctures brain by accidentally ramming car antenna up left nostril,

Say: Toronto Blue Jay kills seagull with homer,

and a deep, indecorous chortle will rise from his belly and burble up his throat and out of his mouth, masking the thin, prissy whine of the fluorescent lights for a few seconds. His laughter is steam—it scalds and leaves something sulfurous in its wake.

Just don't ask him about his daughter who lives a few miles away in Coquitlam and whom he's not allowed to see. And she's only three, so E-mail is not an option.

The Pumpkin usually sits to the left of you and is what they call a lifer. He's been here for longer than anyone can remember and perhaps thinks that if he just keeps really quiet, he can stay forever. The Pumpkin has seven children and a wife to feed. He has beautiful, long eye-lashes—as do all his children—and for some reason those eyelashes break your heart.

The Pumpkin is kind. The Pumpkin is inoffensive. The Pumpkin, you realize, might as well wear a sign reading: Kick Me.

Pick a day, any day. "Hey, Murray," Dave says. "Do you think they should let the U.S. extradite those two pricks from the island who killed the one guy's parents and retarded sister in Bellingham?" The Pumpkin stops, his fingers raised above his keyboard, looking uncertain. "Sure, Dave. I guess they deserve it."

The Matador scoops the puck. "But, Murray, you know they'll probably fry. Don't you Catholics believe guys shouldn't fry on earth, only after they're booted out of heaven?" This is where the Pumpkin starts to sweat and looks around for moral support. You try to flash him a look of concern, smiling wryly and winking, but he just thinks you're flirting and turns even redder. "You're right, maybe we should keep them here."

Dave says, "Right, Murray. Make them do fifty push-ups or ten Hail Marys or something." Now the Pumpkin smiles a watery smile, thinking he's said something witty, and then sees the smirk on Dave's face and the disdain on the Matador's. He hurries to the bathroom while everyone, including you, snickers. The Pumpkin spends a lot of time in the can summoning the strength to do his job.

Start to say: You guys—

Then remember: Nietzsche.

Decide he's in there turning into superman and that he might just come out and bash in everyone's head. Wish that your look of empathy had been less wishy-washy, more distinct. Vow to practice blinding glances of compassion in front of the bathroom mirror on your break, if you're not too tired.

What does it take to push a man over the edge? Nine out of ten disgruntled U.S. postal workers agree: Not a whole heck of a lot.

Consider circumstances under which you might kill. Imagine you have a daughter—seven? strawberry blonde but has begged for highlights? My Little Ponies™ are strewn all over the hallway and you tripped on one earlier that day and twisted your ankle and whaled on her. And during a party a man—a friend's friend's friend? uninvited? jovial uncle? choirmaster? blond monster in nice khakis and Florsheim shoes? high school dropout beaten by stepfather and driven mad by the Scott Joplin tune that spews incessantly from the speakers of the ice-cream truck he drives due to reduced opportunities (he really wanted to be a vet, loves animals, it truly broke his heart)?—enters her bedroom. Seconds later you stand in the doorway and see him burrowing under the covers behind her. You return, limping because of the ankle, with a meat cleaver—still flecked with minced cilantro from the guacamole you made for the party?—and chop off his head, surprised at your own strength. Surprised it was so easy. Thinking about it now, grit your teeth so hard your jaw just about cracks. Wonder what would be a worse trauma for this unknown daughter: the rape itself or the head—the neck a bloodied stump—rolling to the centre of the bed and her mother standing above, wild-eyed, a Chinese meat cleaver in her hand?

To know you would readily kill—to have considered the possibilities—brings a grim relief.

At least you don't call guys like that *Mister* here like they do in the *Globe and Mail*. *Mr.* Olson. *Mr.* Bernardo. *Mr.* Lepine. *Mr.* Karadzic. And *Miss* or *Ms.* Homolka, is that one lump or two? You don't know what you'd do if you had to do that, probably want to quit. Probably wouldn't, though. Just like your compadres there in Toronto don't quit over it. But don't think it doesn't bother them. Rim pigs dream in Technicolor.

Week Five: Learn to look death in the face and laugh. Remember: Rim pigs don't cry.

The formula for what you do here is simple. You could call it the slide rule of tragedy. Take the number of dead and divide it by the number of miles the site of the disaster/murderous rampage/political upheaval lies from the epicentre—which in your case is Vancouver. Then multiply the figure by the importance of that place or the dead to your readers on a scale of zero to ten (this last part is subjective, of course). For example, a plane crash in South America would have to involve at least fifty dead to make it into the paper with three column inches at best. A plane crash up north may get three column inches on page A6 even with only two dead. A plane crash at the Abbotsford Airshow, one dead, makes fourteen column inches on the front page. Two dead in Azerbaijan due to rock slide, well, that wouldn't even make the wire if they're Azerbaijanis. A Burnaby couple killed in Azerbaijan due to rock slide? Now you're cookin' with gas!

You do get bonus points for ironic circumstances. For example: Fitness guru dies of heart attack. Eighty-eight killed in Punjabi village by flooding dam during feast day celebrating opening of said dam.

You could say that you do body counts in inches here, and that's all you do.

Strangely, you wake up most afternoons to find your pillow covered with big, wet blotches. Decide you were drooling. Try to remember your dreams. Even if you can't remember the specifics, you're aware they're always filled with a weird chiaroscuro effect. That's the essential difference between those who dream in their sleep during the day and those who sleep and dream at night, this razzle-dazzle mix of light and shade to create an illusion of depth. All that, *and* Technicolor, especially when it comes to blood and auras.

Bodies plummeting through water in chiaroscuro light, feet encased in cement—or is that concrete?—blocks. Bodies piled by the shed like cordwood in chiaroscuro darkness, still too green to burn. And you, you're the one with the measuring tape and the maniacal laugh.

Week Six: See Week Five

Week Seven: Take in a photo to make your desk area more homey. But remember, it's not really *your* desk, so don't forget to put it away in your mail slot at the end of your shift. It's tough to decide whose photo to bring. A picture of your boyfriend will just remind you of what you're missing and how this job is ruining your life. You have no nieces or nephews. Your brother's never caught a big, huge fish. You have no dog. You decide on Pamela Anderson Lee. This will remind you that things could be worse. You could be a perky, supernatural blonde bombshell who no one in their right mind would make the subject of a visual essay. This way, at least, you stand a slim chance.

The Matador raises his eyebrows. Decide he's kind of attractive at a certain angle in a wan, androgynous way.

Say: I like her, okay?

Say: It's just so you don't confuse us. Ha ha.

Say: Kidding!

Your bra, on the inside of your T-shirt, feels saggy.

The explosion comes in the middle of the week at about 3:00 A.M. There's a dull boom that you barely notice because it comes from so far away. Later you'll remember thinking that it sounded like the nine o'clock gun, but, of course, it couldn't be since it was nowhere near nine o'clock.

It's the sirens everyone reacts to and soon all the phones in the newsroom are jangling. Martin, the young guy from the *Delta Mirror* they brought in to replace the ambitious Anny who's now on courts, is going nuts. He doesn't know which phone to pick up. He runs to the windows to look outside, which is stupid, you think, since the only view is of the back parking lot.

Pick up the nearest phone. Take notes. Realize that you, too, can be a reporter. Anyone can. Just take down the facts, Jack. And don't forget to ask if there were any fatalities. But this is harder than it sounds. You just can't form the word "dead" in your mouth. But there's always hurt—hurt is easier.

Say: I've got the scoop. It's at Broadway and Cambie.

Say: A pizza parlour blew up.

Say: There's glass everywhere.

When Dave asks who you were talking to, force yourself to be honest.

Say (quickly): I don't know.

The Matador's laugh rises up sharp, hot, sulfuric.

Riding the Broadway bus home at 7:30 A.M., you find that the street has already been largely cleared. Workers are putting new plate-glass windows up at the Royal Bank, while small business owners are busy measuring, taping, sweeping, up and down the block. Enormous piles of glass are heaped on the sidewalks and sparkling mounds line the gutters like some dangerous new drug.

Decide to ring the bell and get off the bus even though it's not your stop and your brain is zinging with fatigue, the skin pulled tight across your temples. All that glass is mesmerizing. It looks positively Arctic. Forget the summer heat for a moment and stroll along as if you're on a polar expedition. Stand on a large slab of cracked blue glass and imagine you're an Inuit grandmother sent off to die on her very own ice floe. Decide the idea sounds peaceful. Think about how quiet it would be, lulled to sleep by the waves sluicing across your hands and feet, the ice cracking imperceptibly beneath you as you drift off to sea. All those other worn-out grannies floating on the water.

Try not to be embarrassed when the woman from the Label Clippers store shakes you awake and flags you a cab. Brush slivers of glass nonchalantly from your jeans with a crumpled chocolate bar wrapper.

Back at work, several miles away, the windows are intact. The glass on the picture of Pamela, tucked away in your mail slot, has a hairline fracture, invisible to the human eye.

Week Eight: Resist the temptation towards melancholy. This will be difficult, but not impossible. Very difficult, but not quite impossible. Okay, formidable. But you're a big girl with lots of outer defences. A regular rhino skin. Ex-Catholic, ex-virgin, ex-dreamer, ex-fighter pilot. All these exes make for great epidermis.

You have grown somewhat preoccupied by death in these waning days of summer. Your childhood best friend's mother dies of a disease she shouldn't have had. Lung cancer. A woman who's never smoked a cigarette in her life. Must have been from all those chemicals she was breathing in all those years of cleaning other people's toilets, your mother tells you. You never knew. She lived in a beautiful big house in a leafy subdivision with her husband and three children. A Fisher-Price life. An immigrant's dream. She could afford to have someone come and scrub her own toilet, stick their head in her Jenn-Air. You find yourself in a parking lot outside the Arts Club Lounge on Granville Island howling at the cloud-shrouded moon.

Your soon-to-be-ex-boyfriend says: "Get up. You're drunk." Which is somewhat true.

Tell him: "This is true grief. I'm howling at the moon to mourn, okay?"

These are full-blown werewolfian howls. Your throat aches and you fully expect thick hairs to sprout from the backs of your hands. You later wonder how you got those little bits of gravel embedded in your knees.

Your eyes glow green when you cry this much and the next day you walk the streets with alien orbs, chewing over the mutability of human life, wondering why the rocks that spin out from under the rear wheels of cabs accelerating too quickly at intersections don't puncture veins in fragile necks—the fragile necks of those you love and your own fragile neck in particular—forgetting that rim pigs don't cry. You pass the Sweet Marie Variety and through the window you see the owner's little girl— the one with the deadly straight bangs—sitting on the counter by the cash register, trying to balance a spoon on her nose. You want to tell her to keep practising because life is the ultimate balancing act.

Mouth advice at her through the glass: Don't eat yellow snow. Don't take any wooden nickels. Don't clean other people's toilets. And don't mess around with Jim. Somehow this makes you feel better.

During the night, at work, things are easier. But during the day, death lurks in every corner of your dreams. A friend comes out of the shadows at twilight in a green Austin Mini to pick lilacs from your garden for her eighty-five-year-old father—to bring him back from confused anger to gentle lucidity. She doesn't tell you this. You just know. He rages in your closet, garbled animal noises. You can't make out what he's saying, but you know he wants to die. You clip the lilacs like big clumps of grapes and your friend leaves with an armful, their smell sweetly sickening. You wake up to the crackle of foil and the whoop of a car alarm from up the street somewhere.

Phone your mother long-distance every day, twice a day sometimes—just to say hi—until she asks, "What are you, nuts?"

Across the alley, the staple-gun guys are oddly silent. No show tunes, no rat-a-tat-tat. And it's 2:00 P.M., past their lunchtime and well into the most cacophonous part of the day. You wonder if the house is done, ready to receive its owners, bright young things with lots of money who will sleep peacefully under exquisite percale sheets—240 threads per inch—on the former post-apocalyptic playground. Look out your kitchen window just in time to witness a terrifying sight. One of the men, the youngest—honestly, he couldn't be more than sixteen—is standing on the newly finished chimney, arms extended. You can't see his face, but you can see the sharp little shoulder blades sticking out of his sweaty back like the beginnings of wings. He sways a little. One man carefully straddles the roof, holding his right arm out to the boy, saying something soothing that you can't quite hear, while the rest wait on the ground. You notice that the sky behind them drips like molten lead, clouds churn, fingertips touch in chiaroscuro light, thunder claps—applause from on high for a moment brought to you by Michelangelo.

Say: Whew, it's just a dream.

Say (trying not to sound clichéd): But it seemed so real.

Say—

Just then the man trying to save the boy slips, sending cedar shakes into the air, and a man on the ground, who looks like he could be his brother, screams, "Tony!" in a way that is anything but dreamlike.

Week Nine: Realize that this is more careening than careering.

The photograph, of a skinny man in a cheap cardigan, is the kind of thing you've been trying to avoid. You've been doing the unthinkable—cherry-picking—and you haven't been caught yet. You've been deft, but you've mostly been lucky. A sleepy item on Senate reform; a quirky tidbit on virtual spelunking (Caving for Claustrophobics!); a gushy feature on the reunion of twin sisters separated for forty-five years who find each other through a recipe club specializing in marshmallow dishes—a testament to the resilience of the human spirit, brought to you by Kraft. Those are the kinds of things you can handle. But here it is, the first thing you grab, a face, the face of Matias Zupan, grieving Slovenian father, a face that speaks for the wounded. Matias Zupan, a bony fellow of indeterminate age in a cheap cardigan, a garment so unlike a decent sweater that you have to wonder where it came from. Perhaps it was sent by a harried relation—a guilt-ridden second cousin? younger brother?—who's now in Hamilton. He saw the writing on the wall and left the day after Tito died and now is successful enough with his dry-cleaning business? janitorial service? pizza joint? to be able to send pillowcases full of clothes from Honest Ed's to those he left behind. But trying to make a story of it, making light, doesn't change anything. Matias Zupan, in a carefully knotted tie, contorts his face in anguish. He is held up by two other men at a graveside, his toes, in old Adidas, barely skimming the ground. You slip it under the newspaper on your desk, this obscene portrait of grief, but not before touching the tip of your pinkie finger to the man's lips. Overhead, the fluorescent lights sing. One tube flickers, then pops.

There's a telephone call for you way across the room, at the entertainment desk for some reason. It can't be your soon-to-be-ex since he knows which number to call. Your heart tumbles around like a crazed acrobat as you cross the newsroom in slow motion, wondering why the worst phone calls come in the middle of the night.

It's your mother. You ask what's happened, your nerves jangling.

She says: "I'm just calling to say hi."

You don't respond.

She laughs: "Hi, hi, hi!"

She says: "It's about your father."

But your father, and this is a fact, has been dead for seventeen years.

Back at your desk which is not really *your* desk, someone's moved the newspaper and the photograph of the skinny man at his son's graveside lies exposed at your elbow. His pants are so sharply ironed that you can see the fine crease even in this poor wire copy. Did his wife cry as she ironed them? Are the tears pressed into the slacks? Did she iron to erase the ache in her heart? You know that under the same circumstances you couldn't iron. You couldn't plug it in. You couldn't get the crease just so. You can't even iron under the best circumstances. The tears charge forward, undammed, damned, unstoppable. They shoot from your fingertips and pour from your ears.

As the ground drops away, you crawl into Matias Zupan's mouth, so wide and welcoming in its grief. All of you fits easily inside the cavity of his body. Here in the dark it feels good to lie quietly for long minutes, listening to his breath and yours, trying to get your breathing in sync with his, but you're always a little off. As if his is the real thing and yours just the echo. Light a candle and look around. His rib cage gleams in the flamelight. It's stunningly fragile and beautiful, like forbidden ivory. You're the ship in the ship in the bottle. Run your tongue over his ribs. They taste like tar.

After that, just sit and watch the wax drip onto your hand and listen to the fluorescent lights out there, somewhere overhead, faintly sizzle and hiss.

The Nature

of Pure Evil

Hedy reaches for the telephone to make another bomb threat. In minutes, from the corner windows of this office on the nineteenth floor of the TD Tower, she will see people empty like ants from the art gallery across the way. Last week it was her own building, the week before an entire city block—including the Hotel Georgia, Albear Jewellers and the Nightcourt Pub—and before that the Four Seasons Hotel. She knows it's illegal, but has convinced herself that it's not wrong, nor even harmful. It's a disruption of commerce, nothing more. Even the city gallery, with its reproductions shop and elegant little café, is a place of commerce. Hedy is like Jesus in the temple, screaming, "Get out!"

Only, Jesus most likely wasn't seized with mirth after ordering the people out of the temple. Although Hedy's major acquaintance with the Saviour is not by way of the Bible, but through the rock opera *Jesus Christ Superstar*, she can well imagine that Jesus didn't shake with uncontrollable laughter after knocking over tables of dovecotes and chasing the money-changers and their customers into the street. And what would Jesus think of the temples of today anyway, some of them as violently rococo as the court of the Sun King, shamelessly passing their gilded collection plates at every opportunity? Her next target would be Christ Church Cathedral, no question about it.

Hedy has to admit that her original impetus for disrupting daily commerce had not been half so noble as Jesus's. His was the sanctity of prayer. Hers was Stanley.

Hedy ironed the pleats of Stanley's white tuxedo shirt as he stood in the kitchen alcove in his undershirt, shaking Nuts 'n' Bolts into his mouth from the box and trying not to get any onto his freshly creased tuxedo pants. Hedy lifted the iron and it hissed like a small dragon. She pressed it down one more time. Stanley came over and traced her spine lightly with his hand. "That's perfect, honey. Bang-on job."

After Hedy helped adjust Stanley's bow tie, she asked him one more time, "So how come I don't get to come to this wedding with you?"

"Aw, Hedy, come on. Don't start with that again."

"I'm not starting with anything. It just seems funny."

Stanley shrugged. "I told you, I'm the only one invited."

"In that case, we'll see who has a better time. I'm going to curl up with a fat novel, my box of Quality Street and some Bessie Smith. I hate borscht, anyways."

"Atta girl," Stanley said and chucked her affectionately under the chin.

The next day, Hedy showed up at work with swollen eyes bulging like tennis balls. Tiny blood vessels had burst in her nose from a night of crying. "Allergies," Hedy said brightly in response to the receptionist's concerned look. Brigit, the salesperson at the next desk who had taken it upon herself to become Hedy's best friend, took one look at her and led her into the Ladies. When Hedy told her Stanley had come home after the wedding, packed a suitcase and left because it had been his *own* wedding, Brigit put her hands over her mouth and looked liked she'd stopped breathing.

"Oh, Hedy!"

"It's all right," Hedy sniffed.

"It's terrible. It's so weird. He must be insane."

Hedy shook her head. "He's quite normal."

"If he's not crazy, then he's pure evil."

Hedy looks to see if there's anyone within hearing distance and then starts to dial. At the time management company she works for, the employees pride themselves on organizing their days effectively, conquering gridlock of the mind. They talk of things like Time Bandits and the Time Crunch Decade. By prioritizing their activities, they are seldom stuck working at their desks through the lunch hour. Instead, they are at liberty to go shop for the perfect wedding gift, pick up their dry cleaning, or stroll the mall, a hot dog in hand, pretending to be free spirits while dodging skateboards piloted by heavily pierced and tattooed waifs. As a result, there is usually no one in the office at the tail end of the lunch hour, except for the substitute receptionist and employees organizing house parties who don't want to be caught squandering company time.

The first time Hedy called in a bomb threat, she did it without any forethought. She was on the telephone to a potential client, a paint wholesaler, on the verge of selling him a seminar package for his office staff, when through the big plate-glass windows of the nineteenth floor she saw Stanley walk into the Four Seasons, arm in arm with a woman. She was sure it was Stanley. His red bomber jacket, his bouncy gait. This was one week after she had carefully ironed his white tuxedo shirt and sent him off to his own wedding. The iron had hissed with that reassuring sound she loved. She had even straightened his bow tie.

She told the potential client that a colleague had just collapsed—heart attack, cholesterol, angina, epilepsy, fish bone—it was hard to see from where she was sitting, and she had better go. Her St. John Ambulance training might be needed. Hedy surprised herself with her quick, bubbly lie. She had always been the carefully honest one, the one who admitted to the bus driver that her handful of change was a penny short of the fare, the one who had always come home at least half an hour before curfew.

Her throat tightened at the thought of Stanley taking his bride to lunch at Chartwell. They had gone to Chartwell, once, after they first moved in together. The tomato-gin soup had tickled her nose and Stanley had made a big show of choosing a martini "like Roger Moore would of drunk." In that dark room, with fox-hunt wallpaper and sturdy chairs upholstered in tapestry, Hedy had imagined they were now legitimately in love. What if Stanley and his bride, his *wife*, now sat at the same table, toying with the same cutlery? What if his wife put the very same silver fork into her mouth that Hedy had used to pierce the crisp skin of her stuffed quail seven years ago?

Hedy opened the telephone book, looked up the Four Seasons, and dialled.

She had been surprised how easy it was. People pouring out onto Georgia and Howe streets, dodging traffic and then standing, craning their necks from across the road, waiting for the explosion. The police cars and fire trucks whirring up from all directions, and Hedy standing alongside her colleagues who anxiously lined the office windows wondering what in the world was going on down there. She had pinched her forearms to keep from laughing. All those people milling around on the sidewalks, scared, excited, all because of her one little phone call. And there was Stanley, standing by himself in the crowd, practically right below her window, goosenecking for a better view, his new bride momentarily forgotten.

The newspapers wrote righteous and relieved editorials about the false alarm. But Hedy realized that people had enjoyed the incident. They got to go home and say, "You wouldn't believe what happened today!" People had something to discuss while they waited at bus stops and SkyTrain stations. They were *talking* to each other. By casting them out into the street, Hedy had done them all a favour. Like Jesus.

As Hedy's best friend, Brigit felt compelled to launch a crusade to prove Stanley was evil. Whenever Hedy insisted Stanley had never been the slightest bit crazy, Brigit said, "Then he must be pure evil. There's no other explanation for that kind of behaviour." Hedy found her friend's efforts on her behalf embarrassing. Brigit would haul her up to a colleague's desk and say, "Tell Tina/ Shaffin/Morgan/Pascal, et cetera, exactly what Stanley did." After Hedy finished the *Reader's Digest* version, with much prodding from Brigit, Brigit would say, "Now, don't you find that insane?" The colleague would agree, after glancing at Hedy, that yes, Stanley's actions sounded a touch insane. "But if he's not crazy, then what?" Brigit would ask. "If he's perfectly normal, wouldn't you say he was pure evil?"

Brigit showed Hedy magazine articles about people without consciences—people who, on a mere whim, crushed children's heads like melons, sold fake and fatal remedies to the elderly, or were secretly polygamous. None of them showed any remorse. "It's not just the deed itself, it's the lack of remorse that makes them evil," Brigit said.

It was true Stanley had shown no remorse. "Gotta go, kiddo, Steph's waiting in the car," he had said as Hedy handed him his folded shirts, which he carefully laid into the largest of their burgundy Samsonite bags, along with a handful of the fresh-smelling cedar eggs they kept in the underwear drawer. The luggage was a gift from her mother, who had felt sorry for them when they showed up at the airport one Christmas years ago with their clothes in an old Adidas hockey bag mended with silver duct tape. Hedy considered the set of luggage theirs as opposed to just hers. That's what happens with things after you live together for seven years. She had wanted to ask what "their" song had been at the wedding. She need-ed to know it wasn't their song, Rod Stewart's "You're in My Heart, You're in My Soul." She sort of doubted it— Rod Stewart didn't seem to be held in high regard these days. Still, some things remain sacred.

She wanted to ask whether Steph—or was it Stephanie? —knew about her, but she realized of course she must; he's up here packing his clothes and has asked her to wait downstairs. Hedy had felt giddy, almost hurrying him along, thinking, *His wife's waiting downstairs*, as if she was anxious not to be labelled the other woman, some dame spread-eagled across the bed in filmy lingerie, cooing B-movie enticements.

Hedy had wanted to ask him why he was doing this. But she believed that if he knew, he probably would have told her.

"Hitler, Clifford Olson, David Koresh, those blond monsters in St. Catharines, all anonymous albino hitmen everywhere," Brigit said, "and Stanley."

Hedy has it all down pat now. If she's not creepily specific, this may be the time they decide the caller is crying wolf. They might call her bluff. But then, perhaps they can't afford to take that chance. Not with all those children in the art gallery, Hedy thinks, the ones there for the regular Wednesday children's tour.

Last time, she detailed the type of bomb and the group responsible, which resulted in an even quicker evacuation and a SWAT team—*a SWAT team!* The entire TD Tower and adjoining mall had been emptied out. They weren't allowed to take the elevators, for fear that might trigger the bomb, so everyone in the tower trooped down the stairs, some barely concealing their panic, others skeptical and cursing about sales they'd be losing to competitors. As Hedy was jostled down the stairs, she thought of the adulterers who might not be at work that day due to an illicit rendezvous at Horseshoe Bay or the Reifel Bird Sanctuary. "Bob!" "Sue!" their innocent loves would say when they arrived home. "I was so worried about you because of that bomb threat. I tried to phone but all the lines kept ringing busy." The adulterers, still in a postcoital haze, would let slip, "Bomb threat? What bomb threat?" And the cat, claws and all, would tumble out of the bag.

"Plastic explosives," Hedy says to the hysterical gallery attendant on the other end of the line. "Even trained dogs can't smell them." She knows enough to keep it short so the call can't be traced. Last week the employee who answered the phone at the TD branch downstairs had maintained the presence of mind to try to keep her on the line. "I have two little children," the woman had said. "Louise and Adrienne, two lovely girls. Do you happen to have any children, ma'am?" Hedy had hung up, admiring the woman's outward calm.

But this giddy gallery attendant has already dropped the receiver and is yelling something wildly in the background. Hedy hears the receiver bump against the counter, once, twice, three times, and pictures it dangling on the end of its line, twisting a little like a freshly hooked fish. Someone picks up the receiver and Hedy hears the carefully varnished tones of a Kerrisdale matron, "Who do you think you are?"

Didn't Jesus say, Let he who is without sin cast the first stone? Everyone knows that from their elementary school catechism. And Hedy, well, she is without sin. She is the lamb.

"It's not like it was the love affair of the century," Hedy told Brigit. "We were just comfortable."

"That's still no excuse to treat you like that."

Hedy and Brigit entered the Frog & Peach, a lovely, rustic little French restaurant on the west side of the city.

"These women you're about to meet, they're very good people," Brigit said. "You'll like them. You spend way too much time alone. Women need female friends."

"Please promise you won't bring up Stanley."

Brigit made as if she was zipping up her mouth with her fingers and then tossing the key over her shoulder. She made such a show of it that Hedy could almost hear the key tinkle on the restaurant's terra-cotta tiles.

Hedy had finished her trout with persimmon chutney and sweet potato gratin, and was toying with her fudge cake on raspberry coulis when Brigit brought up the subject of evil. To be fair, she didn't exactly bring it up, but grasped the opportunity when it arose. Mary Tam, who was a French immersion teacher, looked at the praline slice she'd ordered and said, "Oh, *c'est diabolique, c'est mauvais, je l'aime.*" Then she automatically translated, out of habit: "It's devilish, it's evil, I love it."

"Would you say that people who do unspeakable things are plain crazy?" Brigit asked as if the thought just happened to descend on her from the pastoral fresco overhead. Her fork swayed dreamily above her lemon mousse. "Or is there such a thing as pure evil?" Hedy picked up her knife and made a quick sawing motion across her throat. Brigit ignored her.

"It depends on what you mean by evil," said Donna von something, who was unbelievably thin despite her seven-month pregnancy. She had attended university in the States and throughout dinner she fumed about an American professor of hers named Bloom who had decried moral relativism. He had even published a book on the topic, *The Closing of the American Mind*, or something like that. When Hedy weakly joked that she thought the American mind was already closed, Donna had looked at her with pity.

"What's evil in some cultures isn't considered evil in others." Donna's tone implied she would mentally thrash all dissenters.

"By evil, I mean doing something that causes irreparable pain or harm to innocent people," Brigit said. "I don't think it's relative at all."

"Female circumcision. That's brutal any way you look at it."

"Please, I'm still eating."

Mary put down her fork and took a big swallow of red wine. "Hurting children is evil, rape is evil, eating people is evil."

"What if you eat someone to survive, like those rugby players that crashed in the Andes? And look at how curious everyone was, wanting to know what it tasted like." Hedy thought Donna's smile looked wickedly jejune, as if she had just scored a point at a high school debating tournament.

"When you've come into contact with pure evil, there's no mistaking it," Claudia, a practising family therapist, said slowly. She had been rather quiet all through dinner and now the unexpected sound of her voice commanded attention. "When I was living in Ottawa a few years ago, I went to an open house one Sunday. It was a beautiful place in Sandy Hill, right near the University of Ottawa. A three-storey sandstone, with enormous red maple leaves brushing against the front windows because it was fall."

"Fall in Ottawa is fabulous," Brigit said. Everyone shushed her.

"It was full of people, and the real estate agent had put out a platter of petits fours and was serving coffee in real china cups. It felt like some exquisite afternoon salon as people wandered in and out of rooms, chatting, sipping at coffee and nibbling little cakes. But there was this one room on the third floor, sort of an attic bedroom, that people seemed to walk out of really quickly. They came hurrying down the stairs, dribbling coffee and crumbs."

Mary refilled the wineglasses. "I don't know if I can listen to this."

"I went up the stairs behind the real estate agent, who seemed almost hesitant to show me that room. I walked right into it and immediately I felt the hairs rise on the back of my neck and arms. The real estate agent stood in the doorway, just outside the room, and tried to direct my view out the window toward the Ottawa River. But something made me look up. The ceiling was painted black, with thin red lines connected to form a pentagram."

"Look, the hairs on my arms are standing up right now!" Mary held her thin arms out over the table. The black hairs glistened silver in the candlelight. The hairs on Hedy's arms were rising, too. She felt like she used to at sleepover parties when the girls tried to outdo each other with horror stories just before falling off to sleep. Maybe that's what evil was, just another party game.

Donna looked disdainful. "I find it really hard to believe they wouldn't have painted the ceiling over before attempting to sell such a prime piece of real estate."

"That's what I thought, too," Claudia said. "But I found out they had tried. They went through half a dozen professional painters and a couple of university students. Nobody could stay in that room more than five minutes. There was something evil in there, I could feel it. I've never come across a feeling like that before or since."

"I was talking about evil people," Brigit said, sounding irritated. "Not *spirits*."

Hedy looked up at the fresco and saw a bucolic scene of little satyrs chasing plump nymphs across faux-distressed plaster. The candlelight flicked shadows across it, creating the illusion that the creatures were moving, darting in and out of flames. She thought of Stanley and his bride, Stephanie, tousling on a king-size brass bed with jungle-motif sheets and decided that if Brigit brought up the subject of Stanley she would be forced to tip a burning candle into her lap.

"What about that person who's been calling in all those fake bomb threats?" Mary asked.

"Oh, that person," Brigit said. "That person's just nuts."

"I think we're talking about someone who desperately craves attention. Someone deprived of adequate affection in childhood."

"Original. I don't think you need a psych degree to figure that one out."

"I think it's pretty harmless."

"What if someone gets hurt, gets so scared they have a fatal heart attack right there on the street in front of their building?"

Hedy drifted in and out of the conversation. She thought about her childhood, a textbook case of love and understanding. Pork chops and applesauce, Snakes and Ladders, backyard swing sets, and a mother who hadn't been too embarrassed to hold a snowy white cotton pad in her hand and carefully explain what womanhood had to do with Hedy. She thought about Stanley, her affection for the springy rust-coloured hairs on his chest and his ability to bluster through most awkward social situations in an amiably anti-intellectual manner. But was that love?

"If hurting someone wasn't the intent, I would say it wasn't evil."

"Especially if they're sorry."

"What if they say they're sorry, but they're not."

"It's easy to *say* you're sorry."

"Only God really knows."

"What if you don't believe in God, or any gods?"

"Right."

God could really make people scurry, Hedy thought. God of Thunder, God of Lightning. Raining frogs down from the sky, now there was a feat. Where had she heard that? How could a booming giant like God have had a gentle son like Jesus? But it was always the quiet ones who surprised everyone when they finally opened their mouths to roar, wasn't it? Or perhaps she was putting too much stock in the Jesus of Tim Rice and Andrew Lloyd Webber.

"Evil has nothing to do with what's legal or illegal."

"I agree, I mean, there are so many unjust laws."

"Like which ones, for instance?"

"Always the devil's advocate."

"There's that word again."

"What word?"

"Devil."

"Ha ha."

Hedy stands at the window across the room from her desk, looking out toward the art gallery. A small person with green hair skateboards down the granite steps. The Iranians are there, passing out their pamphlets, counting on the milk of human kindness. Others steal a moment from a busy day to sit on the steps and hold their faces to the sun. She feels happy, although she would never tell Brigit that. In Brigit's judgment, she has every right to feel paralysed with unhappiness, catatonic with indignation. But Hedy has combed her heart and found no detritus, no coiled reddish hairs, no rust flakes.

Brigit would find some fault with happiness, anyways. Yesterday, she showed Hedy a magazine article about a British psychiatrist who thinks happiness should be classified as a mental condition—because it's a highly *abnormal* state of being. The psychiatrist wasn't referring to bliss, but a plain, old-fashioned level of contentment and calm. In which case perhaps Stanley is crazy after all, not evil, because he seemed so happy the last time Hedy saw him, unapologetically happy.

She wonders why people haven't started pouring out of the art gallery yet. It's been almost ten minutes since her phone call, yet there are no signs of panic, no sirens piercing the air, no men in stiff black coveralls stealthily slipping through the side entrances of the gallery, their intricate bomb diffusion kits strapped to their belts. Hedy's mood loses a little of its fine buoyancy. She decides she must make the call again. She glances toward her telephone, but sees that Brigit is back at the neighbouring desk.

"I was just listening to the CBC news in the car," Brigit says, as Hedy roots around in her top drawer for a quarter, "and did you know that there's a trend away from accepting pleas of insanity in cases of aggravated assault? It's an acknowledgement of man's baser instincts. I mean men *and* women, of course." Hedy nods as if she's paying attention, and then smiles as her fingers close around a quarter that's been nesting in a pile of paper clips. She tells Brigit that she's forgotten to pay an important bill and has to run down to the bank for a few minutes, just in case anyone asks. Brigit tut tuts, "Oh, those darn Time Bandits!" and waves her off with a conspiratorial wink.

Hedy starts counting as she enters the elevator, needing to know how long it will take to get back upstairs. She wants to be there in time to watch all the people streaming out of the gallery, the panicked milling around with the merely curious, the emergency vehicles dramatically screeching to a halt, the children noisily demanding to be told what's going on. As she walks through the shiny lobby toward the row of pay phones, Hedy feels positively grand. She is the one without sin striding quickly across the burning desert, thin sandals moulded to her calloused feet, the quarter hot and round and flat in the hollow of her hand.

Anxious Objects

for Dr. Spock, R.I.P.

The child has everything it could possibly want and now it comes to you, this evening after the first day of junior kindergarten, and says, "I'd like some pajamas."

This child who already has a goldfish and rabbits (yet unnamed), a music box with one of those tiny ballerinas that pop up and twirl slowly to *Swan Lake*, a porcelain tea set bearing the likeness of that little Parisienne Madeline, a skipping rope (yet unused), a horse (named Conan, after her favourite late-night talk-show host), her own home page and Internet account, and an Air Miles card boasting 29,342 points; this child who has an indoor speedskating oval (which, you must admit, you and your wife have tried out, once maybe, zipping along feeling like Hans Brinker and his love, cheeks ruddy, hand in mitted hand, though only when the child wasn't around as you would never encroach so aggressively upon the child's *space*); this child who has a safety deposit box containing the following: a chunk of the Berlin Wall, a swatch from the Shroud of Turin, and a signed, first-edition *Tropic of Cancer*; this child who has an older sister, stillborn, whom the child keeps in a jar of formaldehyde hidden away someplace known only to the child (although you suspect she has traded the former with a friend up the street for a Pocahontas poster, but, well, *kids will be kids*); this child of whom you still carry an ultrasound photograph in your wallet from the time before you even knew she would be a she (not that you *cared*), who is the glue that holds your marriage together, who is the indelible ink of your heart, who is now standing in front of you saying that *all* the other children at school have pajamas.

You have, up until now, found it difficult, and largely unnecessary, to deny your child anything. Somewhere up there, invisible to the naked eye, orbits a man-made satellite named in her honour, and it wasn't cheap. Would that it were a planet. But *pajamas*?

What kind of place is this school where children of all races and abilities learn together in harmony and yet claim to *all* have pajamas? (Note: Find out who this Italian pedagogue Montessori really is and what kind of social experiment he or she is up to.) You might as well be sending the child to that public school down the block where syringes litter the schoolyard like space debris and twelve-year-old girls hanging around the sagging metal fence claim to be able to do outrageous things with their sturdy, black-licorice-stained lips.

Isn't there a point in a child's life, in your life together as parents and child, that you have to *lay down the law?*

"Pussywillow, kittycat, caramel corn, l'il Amy March, pigeon pie, Sailor Moon, apple-o'-my-eye," you say, carefully modulating your tone so as to spare the child any distress, "whatever do you need pajamas for?"

Innocently, not aware that she's about to bring the whole sound structure of your Benzedrine-fuelled lives down upon your heads, she leans her face adorably to one side, folds both tiny hands together in a perfect simulacrum of prayer, and presses them alongside her tilted cheek.

"For sleeping," the child says.

And surely as if it were actually happening, the joists in the ceiling groan and the house shifts on its foundations. Plaster dust swirls down chalky and you struggle to see the child through the sudden whiteout, through this authentic, circa 1890s Manitoba snowstorm. The wind howls in your ears, your frostbitten toes and left hand will need amputating. In your arms there's an infant in a coarse saddle blanket who'll be stiff as a board soon, a blue boy. You've only completed grade five. Cows are all you've ever learned anything about, the only thing you're good at, and now they're stuck far out in the fields, the sky lowering down on them. You're Swedish, they won't let you forget. They (they, *them*) say you smell. It is your duty to brood. Your wife, dear God... but right now all you can think, brain hot with jumbled coals, is, *read Dog, save my child.*

But the child is still standing there in front of you in

the kitchen, bathed in halogen light, smiling sweetly, the corners of her mouth smudged chocolatey from an Energy Bar, saying, "For sleeping."

The chamber ensemble you've engaged to accompany all of the child's pronouncements stirs and launches into Schubert's string quartet in D minor, but you abruptly hold up the palm of your hand. The musicians move closer together, chairs squealing against the linoleum, and begin to mutter quietly among themselves, bows across their laps.

These other children *sleep*? When do they have time for ballet and kick-boxing, glass-blowing and oenology, snowboarding and target practice? And what about *citizenship*—staffing polling stations, canvassing door-to-door for the Vancouver Aquarium's new whale pool, and volunteering at St. Paul's Eating Disorders Clinic, not to mention all those guided tours to the sewage treatment plant on Annacis Island? How do they keep up? Can these children do a triple lutz? Can they even drive a four-by-four? Have they climbed K-2 yet (*without* oxygen)?

Upstairs, your wife is on-line, preregistering the child for an undergraduate year abroad at either the University of Strasbourg or the University of Kyoto (playing it safe, as neither of you, even after commissioning an exhaustive poll with a margin of sampling error of +/-3.5 per cent, can predict with any degree of accuracy whether the next century belongs to the new Europe or the Pacific Rim). She is coolly oblivious to the drama unfolding down here in the kitchen. You seek to distract the child. "Let's check with mom, cherry popsicle. Meanwhile, why don't you practise some composition?" The child is currently undertaking the score for an opéra bouffe and appears to have a nice light touch. The chamber players, glancing over her shoulder at the computer screen, have more than once nodded their honest salt-and-pepper heads in approval.

She says she prefers to finish the chess game you started last week. You want to concentrate, give it your best shot, but the queen's knight, as you lower your hand to advance its pawn, flares its nostrils, snorting steam hot enough to scald your fingertips.

Your wife descends half an hour later, looking marvellously thin and fingering the buttons on her blouse.

"Zöe," she says, sitting down on the bottom stair and calling to her daughter. Every day the child has a new name but none of them stick, no name ever seems *le nom juste*. Now you are at the end of the alphabet and must start again. Tomorrow the child will be Amelia or Agnes or Andrea or Aphrodite. And she will react accordingly, trying on the name like a new swimsuit, squirming a little—sometimes in discomfort, sometimes in delight. Tamara was one she liked, but it made her a touch too dreamy for your tastes. Other names make her sweat, like Debbie. "I feel fat," she had complained all day. And hadn't her inner thighs rubbed together a little, her tiny OshKosh corduroys singing like crickets when she walked?

Your wife unbuttons her blouse and the child settles herself into her mother's lap. The child has lost two of her milk teeth already and has grown a snaggletooth. So it was decided last month that braces were in order. The child's smile will be beautiful, but your wife's breasts are a mess of scrapes and hard-blooming bruises. You've discussed weaning the child, but not with any real conviction. You both know that nothing is as good for a child as mother's milk, and nothing is too good for the child. And besides, it keeps your wife's breasts large and the rest of her body thin, which pleases you both.

There was a time, not so long ago, when the space between the two of you was large and growing. At first the size of an audible sigh, then an American-style football field, it became, over the course of a few years, a tundra of migrating caribou which, viewed from above through the window of a turbulent single-engine, resembled a swift, dirty river, but from up close thundered by so loud and hard your heart almost stopped. Now the space between you is the size and shape of one small child, a not unbridgeable distance. For there is always the child to consider. The things it would know. The things it might choose to imagine.

All night long, you and your wife discuss this pajama thing in hushed tones, in hushed *Latvian* tones, as that is the only language, living or dead, that your child has yet to master. Unaware of what is at stake, the child has various feng shui manuals opened up on the living-room rug and is carefully rearranging the furniture in order to maximize the flow of positive *ch'i*. Every so often she implores you to help her drag the Eames chair or the

Nienkämper couch to another location. She's so small and determined that it almost cracks you in two. The various objects, lined up on the mantel, look anxious.

The tired eyes of your wife are a holy purple—like the cloths draped over statues in churches at Easter—and tissue-paper thin. It's true that none of you have slept since the night the child was a giddy blue line in the home pregnancy kit—some four years, eleven months, twenty-three days and six hours ago. A blue line wavering like a mirage that you and your wife regarded together as you sat on the cold edge of the tub and she on the toilet seat, both electrocuted with joy. It's true that you have pouches under your own eyes the size and heft of a kilo of coke and that the skin over your skull feels like Saran Wrap pulled tight and airless. Sometimes, sitting at your desk at work, you'll jerk violently as if breaking a fall, much like you used to do in your sleep, but you won't be sleeping. On the Burrard SkyTrain platform you've visualized jumping, a quick belly flop onto the tracks, just to relieve the pressure in your head. It's true that the child's eyes are so wide sometimes and so glassy that they look like they might just pop out and land in the soup.

The doorbell rings. Your wife yelps, even though the visit isn't unexpected. "I actually *yelped*," she says, forcing a laugh, because the child now looks worried. It's not all the moonlighting you both do that your wife minds, but this. Guys named Dougie and Chin coming to the back door with envelopes of money at 4:00 A.M. You get up, your knees popping stiffly, and go take the package out of the hall linen closet where it's shoved in behind the Christmas table runner, a porridge of guilt assembling in your gut. Your wife folds and unfolds the cuff of her blouse. The child is on tiptoes, reaching for the stars, her whole body vibrating like piano wire.

In the suburbs outside of Tokyo, just across the ocean, the next day's sun is already shining and school-children rain from the sky, their smart little backpacks like parachutes that won't open. They spill off balconies like thread unspooling. They slip through your fingers. They land in your coffee, jangling your nerves.

The child is kneeling on the front windowsill when you get back, looking out into the darkness, silently working her way through the periodic table, her sweet milk breath misting the glass as she mouths the names of the chemicals. The chamber players play Prokofiev's string quartet no. 1 in B minor, music so discordant yet compelling it occurs to you that it could only have come to him in a sea-pitched dream. Your wife folds and unfolds the cuff of her blouse. The door of the hall closet is ajar.

The child turns her head and says, in a voice on tiptoes, vibrating like piano wire, "Radon, a radioactive, gaseous, chemical element formed, together with alpha rays, as a first product in the atomic disintegration of radium: symbol, Rn; at. wt., 222.00; at. no., 86; sp. gr., 973 g/1; melt pt., -71°C; boil. pt., -68°C."

The music folds and unfolds.

Tomorrow, you and your wife just might send the child out with the nanny to find some pajamas.

And tomorrow night, tomorrow night you might turn out the lights, and with your wife pressed to your stomach in one of your old T-shirts, sore breasts leaking, and with you naked because you're always so hot, and with your daughter in her new pajamas (my jammies, she'll call them, already one step ahead of you), all three of you will close your eyes and try very hard to sleep. Just as a lark. To see what it's like.

A child, after all, must be resilient enough to take any curveball life throws at it. But a terrible fear stalks the neighbourhood of your heart, as you think you may be unleashing a force you can't control, some yet undiscovered monster.

Odds that,
all things
considered,
she'd someday
be happy

"But thank God for all those turns in my life,
even the bad ones—maybe especially the bad ones."
—Roman Polanski, *The New Yorker*, December 5, 1994

PROLOGUE

The former teen terrorist, sitting on the back porch—which isn't really a back *porch* as such, but a fire escape overlooking an alley lined with three-foot fennel gone to seed, the deranged beauty of panic weed bursting through a seam in the pavement, graffiti-splattered garbage cans, some so dented by angry ex-boyfriends behind the wheels of circa 1981 Camaros that they look doubled over from a sucker punch (as well as blue boxes heaped with wine bottles, Costco-size Prego jars, and empty four-litre plastic milk jugs because these buildings backing onto the alley house many growing, fatherless children, two of whom wobble by below on second-hand in-line skates pushing at each other and yelling, "Don't be such a fag!")—her bare feet up on the hot metal railing, the two elongated second toes (index toes?) humped like camels from the time, years ago when she was still afflicted with caring *what people thought*, she bought a pair of Frye boots a full size too small, but on sale, and permanently reconfigured her feet between which now, framed in a V and shimmering in the Indian-summer heat, she can see Tibetan prayer flags flutter across the alley on the clothesline of a fuzzy-haired young couple just back from a trek in Nepal, her ringless fingers peeling an orange, the juice spraying lightly across her bare knees, beading them like small gems, finds herself thinking that life couldn't possibly be better.

At this very moment, the girl trekker, the sturdier and fuzzier of the pair (the boy is the one with the delicate frame and high cheekbones, the one who gets propositioned by both men and women outside Yaletown clubs while his patchouli-scented girlfriend studies maps at their seed-strewn kitchen table planning their next escape, the Dalai Lama looking impishly down on her from a steam-wrinkled calendar on the wall) steps outside onto her own porch but not *porch*. With a moon-glow expression, she pitches a rinsed-out tahini sauce bottle in a perfect arc into a blue box below where it explodes with that always teeth-wrenching shatter of glass on glass.

The former teen terrorist's hands spring involuntarily to her ears. Orange squelches against her temple, already matted with sweat, and juice drips down the back of her right ear and along her neck. Like a thin trickle of blood, she can't help but think. Like blood you don't notice until later when you're taking off your shirt and wondering what all that pink around the neckline is before stuffing it, along with all your other clothes from that night, into a garbage bag.

Her ears, they won't stop *ringing*. Through the heavy curtains of heat, through the very weight of the dazzling light, the sound comes to her as if from under water, and it takes a while before she realizes it's the telephone.

I. HERSELF

Herself doing cartwheels across the lawn. The whole world standing by the peony bush applauding. She's so quick her tiny hands and feet ignite small fires, tufts of flame in the grass, while her audience oohs and aahs. "Thank you, thank you very much," she says, lowering her upside-down voice like radio Elvis, "Thank you, thankyouverymuch." Fireworks go off overhead, spelling out her name. She curls her lip as if she doesn't care.

Later, at supper, her mother says, "Sit still, pussycat."

Never, never, never.

Tomorrow, before her mother's even up, herself will cartwheel all the way to somewhere, maybe Nashville, maybe even Gay Paree.

"This place is deadsville," she says, something she heard her kindergarten teacher's hippie boyfriend say.

He made boobs on the little Paki kid's plasticine rabbit (with *nipples*!) and the whole class went berserk right there in the basement of St. Matthew's United Church. Except herself, who kept her cool.

Her mother laughs.

She considers showing her mother the tattoo of her teacher's boyfriend's (soon to be *hers*) initials on her belly. She's penned them on backwards so that she can read them in the mirror.

A little trick she picked up in Shanghai.

Herself—variously known as Panda Bear, pussycat, Miss Molly (as in Good Golly!), Katy Kadiddle, just plain Kate, and Katherine (*Kaw*theryn by her piano teacher who has come from England and personally knows the Queen)—has seen a dead man.

At her recital she plays "Für Elise" with real feeling, knowing that having seen a dead man has changed her forever. The clapping is thunderous, so to show her emotion she bursts into tears. The audience, all the other Royal Conservatory students' parents, can't believe how sensitive she is and they clap even more loudly until she can see there's a danger the roof of this small auditorium might cave in on them. Under her teacher's arm, a chihuahua shivers uncontrollably, its eyes wet and bulging.

Herself on the stage bowing. Not the same girl she was yesterday.

The dead man was lying in the field just outside the barracks at the end of her street, past where the city workers were laying tar on the road. A wasp hovered around the rim of his ear. It was disappointing that he had all his clothes on. She toed his crotch with her bare, tar-caked feet. She pulled his wallet out of his back pocket, smelled the leather, thought she could almost smell something else, distributed the money, just some coins, into the three pockets of her smock top. She sat and stared at him, the longish hairs that hung from his nostrils, the sweat slicked across his forehead, something in the corner of his mouth (a fleck of burnt toast?), and then put a rock across his ear (oh yes!), trapping the wasp.

"Jesus fucking Christ!" The dead man shot up, darkening the sky.

She ran so fast the road smoked under her feet.

So that's what it's like to raise a man from the dead.

Jesus fucking Christ. The words like chocolate-covered cherries in her mouth.

Herself slips a leather barrette into her pocket at The Bay downtown while her mother looks at nylons. The barrette has two holes and a sharp wooden stick to hold her hair in place. It will look great with her new peasant blouse. She already has half a dozen of these things at home, all of them presents from other girls for her tenth birthday last month.

Her mother picks out a pair of two-for-one pantyhose with reinforced toes.

"Those are for old ladies," she tells her mother. "You'll never get a date." She sighs and smiles the crooked smile she knows tightens the crown of thorns around her mother's heart. She wants her mother to be sexy so they can dance together like sisters in the living room to "Waterloo," licking at little squares of paper with Charles Manson's face on them and blowing their minds while the neighbours watch from behind their curtains, stupid with jealousy, thinking, "That Kate can really cook!"

A salesclerk hovers, his breath like hot-dog relish.

She stares at him, looks right into his little piggy eyes without blinking until he's forced to look away.

Herself at the Ice Capades, the costumes so lush and skaters so spectacular her stomach churns and her limbs twitch. The audience is enraptured with a small, blonde, muscular girl with an enormous pink feather headdress who spins like a gyroscope while rows of elegant men fold over like dominoes in her wake. Herself finds the fingers of her right hand convulsing as if pumping a trigger, spraying bullets at the girl.

She stands up on her seat, number 32, row 12, section C, and sways, then crumples to the concrete floor, Coffee Crisp wrapper and spilled Fresca sticky under her cheek. The entire stadium shudders as her body hits the ground. At least a 4.5 on the Richter scale.

"She must have a fever," her mother says, worried hand on her forehead.

They make way for her and her mother and a kindly man who helps support her stumbling through the parted, standing crowd.

The peacock on the ice forgotten. All eyes on her now.

Herself kneeling, heady from the incense and the thick-
ness of the hymns and all that blood she's losing, so pale
now she is sure she positively glows, the cotton pad
between her legs still so unfamiliar. In front of her the
priest is waiting, communion wafer pinched between
thumb and forefinger. She opens her mouth and before
he can pull back his hand she traps his finger between
her lips. Just because she can.

His skin rough and chalky, the finger filling more of
her mouth than she thought it would. She narrows her
eyes at his shock and her own and sucks hard.

The nail pressing up against the roof of her mouth,
but gently, as he slowly pulls his finger out.

Her own spit glistening on the priest's finger as he
reaches for another host and turns from her.

There's a whole row of kneeling people, eyes closed,
softly perspiring. Herself, electric, grinning up at Jesus
who may or may not care what's going on.

Herself straightening the limbs of a severely palsied child.
This is what all the girls are doing, volunteering with the
retarded. It's called citizenship.

The child lies on his back in a bed in a sour-scented
room full of other narrow beds, his knees to his chest,
his elbows by his ears, mouth twisted, spit coursing down
his right cheek in a thin steady stream. She moves one of
his thighs in a small circle at the pelvis, the way the nurse
demonstrated, otherwise the leg could snap. She turns
her head to the side, trying not to look at his face, or her
gorge will rise. Out of the corner of her eye she sees the

child stretch his lips into what could be construed as a smile and his rocking increases in severity.

"Oh, look, he's excited," the nurse says, teasing her from the other side of the bed.

The boy has a hard-on.

"Well, he *is* sixteen and you're a good-looking girl." The nurse winks.

Sixteen, her age. She looks at the grimacing pretzel rocking on the bed and covers her mouth. Vomit creeps up her throat, she swallows it back. Control is everything.

There's some screaming in the corridor and the nurse is off. She reaches for the boy, locking eyes with him, until he comes and groans and screws his eyes shut.

Not even looking at her.

Herself at her desk, staring down at another A-plus, staring until her eyes cross. The teacher beaming at her from the front of the classroom with her large cracked mouth.

Only the second week of grade twelve and already the boredom's a live animal crawling all over her skin, making her so twitchy she has to sit on her hands to keep from clawing herself bloody, jumping up, screaming, *Get it off, get it off, get it off.* Over the intercom she hears her name: *herself, herself, herself.* All around her sit the dumb and the dead, oblivious, scratching hieroglyphics onto paper, doodling their own names, their epitaphs. Passing notes of limited ambitions. *So-and-so wants to fuck you.* The teacher straightening piles of paper on her desk, the concentration needed for this beading her forehead with sweat. The supreme *effort* of it all.

She needs to raise the dead, to blow something to kingdom come. When was the last time she's heard a good burst of anything—fireworks, applause, a man shooting up to the sky, an explosion?

Her thumbnails—moons glowing, cuticles perfectly tamed—press into her palms so hard she breaks skin.

She raises a hand for permission to leave the room.

The teacher smiles benignly at her and nods, not noticing the thin crescent of blood. Her stigmata.

Herself playing with fire.

In an east-side squat she burns wood ticks off the rump of a part-golden retriever, part-something else. What she likes best is the smell of sulfur as she strikes match after match. Or the flame itself. Or the burnt head of the matchstick she crumbles between her fingers and rubs playfully onto the forehead of the guy beside her who sits in yoga position reading a book of collected Doonesbury comics.

Rubs it into the shape of a cross. "Ash Wednesday," she jokes.

The yoga man was at an ashram near Benares. Now he sits and longs for Bodhisattva, this gaunt young satyagrahi.

The two other girls there, older than herself, are anarchists. Pissed off about everything and anything.

On the door of the squat they've spray-painted "EXPOtation" and "World's Fair No Fair!" and "Meat is Murder!" They stomp around in new Doc Martens, leather creaking, talking loudly about what an idiot this guy they used to like is working at McDonald's. Every so often one of them bends down to kiss the dog on the head.

Herself in her corner of the squat, still the A student, studying books by candlelight, all from the Britannia Library up the street: *The Poor Man's James Bond, Molotov & Other Cocktails, The Blaster's Handbook*. One of the anarchists offers to lend her a shoplifting poncho, a pilly brown-and-white thing smelling of creosote and cumin. But she doesn't need camouflage.

She's the original Benday Dot girl. From far away, there she is, solid, bright, with a cartoon smile, bouncing along the street and you would swear that's a tennis racket in her hand, a trophy under her arm, but the closer you get the more disembodied she seems until—hello? A little trick she picked up from a guy from Nazareth.

This way of disappearing right under people's noses.

Herself with an action plan, standing on her grassy knoll, shifting her weight from one hip to the other.

The anarchists are easy enough to convince, although they want to know: why Tony's Pizza & Donair, and not McDonald's? Herself on her toes, reeling them in like eager trout. *Think globally, act locally.* Besides, there's no security at Tony's, it's smaller, closes earlier, *and* the owner keeps a Playboy calendar behind the counter. *Sexist pig!* They pace around impatiently, kicking at the walls, looking to her for direction.

All the yoga man has to do is drive the getaway car. "What car?" one of the anarchists asks. Herself buzzing now, already jumping into the burgundy Toyota Cressida with a maple leaf-shaped cardboard air freshener hanging from the rearview mirror that she's seen parked outside the Peter Pan Daycare—day after day at 3:30 P.M., key in the ignition, running—and roaring away from the building that's about to blow.

He shakes his head weakly, *no*. He hasn't eaten for eight days to protest some injustice she can't recall. The anarchists, they can't *stop* eating. Being angry just burns up so much energy. They pounce on anything she brings home, only stopping to ask if it has meat in it. She always says no, no meat, of course. A few days ago they ate a couple of jet-hot curried Jamaican patties with ground beef and peas. "With meat substitutes this good," one of them exclaimed, "people only continue to kill animals because we're all just so conditioned by the military industrial complex."

In the middle of the night, she pulls at the divine boy's thin toes. Separates each one gently from the rest and wiggles it. "You can pretend you're a taxi," she says, her voice threading his ear, "just cruising along looking for one last fare."

"It just doesn't seem very pacifist," he says. "I've been trying really hard.

"But I can't drive," he finally tells her after she scrambles over him, tattooing his limbs with her mouth.

Herself crashing through the brush near Squamish with her swami while helicopters rattle by so low overhead they flatten the treetops. His hand, which she grips, is remarkably dry; his thin, diaper-like pants billow out, catching in the branches, and they stumble, slipping to the ground on wet pine cones. "What have we done?" he breathes, almost crying, as megaphones thunder their garbled names across the sky. Her nose is up against his neck, and caught in the crosshairs of her vision are a spray of birthmarks that spell out her name.

"You are a lovely boy," she whispers.

The one true thing she has ever said.

Only this is a dream.

Just one week later he will be a human potato chip, lying on oiled plastic sheets at St. Paul's so no more skin will peel off, the machinery whirring all around him determined to keep him alive so that he might face the music, this silver-tongued Svengali, as the news reports will call him, with no lips left with which to tell his story.

This part is not a dream.

Herself alone on the street in the leaky silence between the explosion and the sirens, the streetlights shattered, casting no shadow.

Getting up from where she's been thrown to the ground and running, her own footsteps echoing in the hollow of her throat.

The car, empty childseat in the back, entombed in a woof of heat, sealed tight, skinny man's hands gripping the wheel at ten and two o'clock, just the way he'd been taught by her that afternoon. Foot forgetting which pedal was the gas.

Herself at her trial, remembering to sit up straight, breathe slowly through her nose. She's sure she's never felt more controlled, more in charge of herself, than at this moment when her name is on everyone's lips. A thin whisper. Like a consecrated host.

The two anarchist girls—who had chickened out at the last minute, forcing her to go into the all-night store at the corner of Venables for a pack of matches that the woman actually made her pay for because she wasn't buying anything else—can't look at her. That elephant-sized woman, the mother of the girl who died in the blast, who is drawing attention away from herself with her undignified, spasmodic weeping, just won't *stop* looking at her. Peeling the skin from her bones with her big watery eyes.

But her own mother won't even look at her.

This is how she thinks she'll remember her mother years from now: frozen-faced, in profile, defeated by bad odds. Her mother, stuck in a time warp in front of a big, industrial-strength adding machine that shudders on her desk as she bangs in numbers that print out on a tight, seemingly endless roll of white paper. The paper curls onto the edge of the desk in a quivering mound before tumbling onto the floor. Her mother, bent over, tongue running back and forth in concentration across already receding lower gums, trying to determine the odds that her daughter is alive and well, the odds that she'd ever see her again, the odds that, all things considered, she'd someday be happy.

II. HER VICTIM'S MOTHER

Just before throwing to a Saturn commercial, Dot says, "Remember, the world won't heal unless we do." Her tag line. She waves her hand, "See you tomorrow." Her smile cracks the crust of her face. The red lights on cameras one and two blink off.

"Dorothy," someone calls from the studio audience. Dot's smile peels back off her teeth as she peers into the stands. Someone from the old days—everyone calls her Dot now, or rather, "Dot!", a tiny perfect name for the tiny perfect talk-show host she has become. There's one at almost every taping. People way back from high school days in Haney, mothers of old boyfriends, customers from the Broadway Supervalu, her former boss. Him she wanted down on his hands and knees, pants down around his ankles, a flaming whip in her hand smartly snapping the air as she pressed the heel of her cream-coloured Frenghetti pump slowly into his right eye. Instead, she opened her arms wide (the same arms that had held disgraced politicians, wife beaters, tree spikers, pimps, arsonists, dealers, fraud artists, clear-cutters, a former leader of the Aryan Nations, a triad member, and a Catholic bishop who had liked native girls a little too much) while he stood there nervously picking at his teeth with an expired lotto ticket until his beaming wife gave him a shove right into Dot's embrace. No meat-locker boner this time, pal? Dot thought. Whassamattah, cat got your Oscar Mayers? By the time she'd released him his fear smelled winegum sour.

"Dorothy Hay." In front of her stood one of Gloria's old high-school teachers, a tall woman Dot remembers as a nervous Nellie, her fingertips continually smoothing her throat as she spoke. This woman had once implied that Gloria might well be a little retarded. She hadn't actually come out and said it. She used the lingo. Difficulty grasping simple concepts. No spatial skills. Inappropriate laughter. She suggested Gloria might be better off at a special school. Then, as delicately as she could, she tried to explain how Gloria sometimes sat at her desk completely preoccupied with the contents of her nostrils—playing with them, *even ingesting them*. She said Gloria's activities made her the scapegoat of all of the grade tens.

"Are you saying my kid eats her snot?" Dot, then still Dorothy, asked. The teacher nodded, her fingers scrabbling at her throat as if she were trying to untangle a knot. Dorothy had gone home and tried to beat the shit out of Gloria, chasing her around the townhouse with a wet dishrag. But Dorothy, with almost 185 pounds back then on her five foot two frame, wasn't much for running those days. "You hate me!" Gloria screamed. And Dorothy, panting against the fridge, wiping her face with the dishrag, hadn't answered.

Now this teacher stood in front of Dot, proposing a memorial to mark the tenth anniversary of Gloria's tragic death. "Something delicate," the teacher says, "in keeping with her sensitive spirit." Her fingers are nowhere near her throat and Dot's not sure if this is in fact the same woman. "She loved nature," the teacher continues, "so I'm thinking a tree. A silver birch."

She loved nature? Dot wants to snort. The nearest Gloria ever got to nature was squashing carpet beetles against the floorboards in her bedroom with her thumb.

"We would have a dedication ceremony. The girls are very into things Celtic these days, so I'm thinking something with Druids, like at Stonehenge but without all that nudity, of course. And one of our mothers makes these little chocolates in the shape of Haida characters—the frog, the raven, the whale. We could pass those around. She's not actually native herself, but they look *very* authentic." Dot wonders whatever happened to Rice Krispie squares.

"We would extend an invitation to all of Gloria's old classmates, those who still live in the Lower Mainland. They were very traumatized when it happened. I'm sure some of them still have nightmares." Oh yeah, Dot thinks, nightmares of Gloria rolling up a great big rubbery one, popping it into her mouth, and then trying to deep-tongue kiss them. Dot would like to get her hands on some of these vicious kids, most of whom have now grown up and no doubt had some vicious kids of their own, tie them behind an eastbound semi like links of sausage and drag them down the Lougheed Highway.

"Maybe we could get that boy, that one in that band, to sing something. *I* know," the teacher's eyes grow wide, as if on cue, "maybe you could have me on your show to talk about all the plans. Then maybe people would even fly in all the way from Toronto!" The woman's hands. That was it. This woman teacher had been a man, a tall nervous man. Dot is suddenly delighted and makes a mental note to ask one of the chase producers to find a slot for the teacher on that upcoming "Dot!" on gender issues and forgiveness.

All around them fans are clamouring for Dot's autograph. And her musky Jōvan-scented embrace.

When the call had come, Dorothy was trying to get some shut-eye after a double shift of bagging groceries at the Supervalu for long, snaking lines of customers who looked like they were on day parole from Oakalla. She was lying over the far edge of the bed with one arm hanging down to the floor, as the middle sagged so badly with her weight the old mattress often threatened to flip up on either side of her to make a Dorothy sandwich. Sweat pooled off her in the freak mid-October heat.

Dorothy had last seen her daughter lounging on the couch with a box of Crackerjacks, watching a video. "Don't stay up too late," she'd said. Gloria said something Dorothy couldn't make out, the kid's mouth was so full of caramel corn. "Chew and swallow before you speak," Dorothy said. This was something Dorothy herself always tried to do, no matter how hungry she felt. She'd chew slowly and swallow and then speak. The first step on the road to thinness and elegance. That and the mid-Atlantic accent she practised in front of the bathroom mirror. Something she learned from an Audrey Hepburn movie, the one with all the singing where Audrey started out poor and a mess, but later wore her hair in a humdinger of a bun like a princess. Dorothy tried to sound both adamant and girlish at the same time. She tried to send friendly fireworks rocketing from her eyes while smiling whimsically, but only managed to look churlish and mildly constipated. What had her mother always said? "Can't make butter with a toothpick." It had meant something at the time.

She lay there in bed waiting and waiting to sleep, the clock radio on the floor beside her flipping its digits so slowly each second felt like a single hair being yanked from her scalp. Her whole life was like that. Like a form of Chinese water torture. Waiting to get thin. Waiting for the bus. Waiting to win a lottery. Waiting for her kid to stop being such a moron. Waiting for the right moment to lock her boss in the meat locker and claim it was an accident.

Later, what she tells people, because that's how she remembers it, is that she picked up the phone before it even rang. A mother knows.

One of the cameramen stops and gives Dot a high-five. She has to do a little hop to even make contact with his hand—she's so short (*petite!*) her lacquered fingernails barely touch his palm. It's their flirty game, but that's as far as it ever goes. In her Dorothy days he was the kind of lanky man she would have given up anything for if he'd even bothered to eyeball her name tag above her left boob when she handed him his change at the check-out counter. The kind of guy who'd look good climbing slowly down a ladder with a toolbelt slung low across his hips. Now he was just another techie and she was... Dot! Although Liz Taylor had married that construction worker, that Larry somebody with the Ukrainian name, who made a big deal about still working after they got hitched (like those lottery winners who say they'll keep on working at the factory, just keep glue-gunning the stripes onto Adidas sneakers or whatever, just because they like the routine, maybe get a new car, something with air-conditioning so they don't drop dead driving to Regina in August for the family reunion).

When Dot gets a break she hangs onto it with both hands, with her teeth if she has to, like those women at the circus who spin in the air with their jaws clamped tight onto a leather strap at the end of a high wire.

On one of the TV monitors, a man and woman slowly circle a car in a showroom. The man peeks through a window and sees a babyseat in the back and then looks over the roof of the car at the woman who's smiling right at him. He circles over to her and swings her around in his arms while all the salespeople and other customers at the Saturn dealership burst into applause.

Dot hates this ad. She hates the woman's downcast eyes, her shy Di half-smile, and the coy way she's picked to tell her husband (yes, they're married of course, her tasteful little ring glints conspicuously as she cradles the telephone receiver while calling the Saturn folks to set up the babyseat-in-the-new-car scheme) that they were going to have a kid. And she especially hates the way everyone applauds as if they'd done anything out of the ordinary that pigs or hamsters or people who don't drive Saturns couldn't do. She should know.

A couple of weeks ago, Dot was in Avanti's, a sports-bar in her old neighbourhood, being interviewed by someone from *Chatelaine* who was doing a profile on her. "When I was a large Marge and thought life sucked a wad," she told him, knowing her fans liked her to be salty but not actually swear, "I used to come down here and play electronic Trivia. Of course, that was before what happened to Gloria."

Beside them, Dot overheard a pregnant woman telling a friend about breaking the news: "I just went to the drugstore and got the kit and told him, 'Just a sec, I'm gonna go pee on the stick.' Then I came out and said, 'See.'" The woman, who had on a spectacularly fringed suede vest with nothing underneath, held up a french fry pocked with gravy to demonstrate.

Her friend clutched her arm, "What did he say!?"

"He goes, 'No way.' So I'm like, "'Yes way.'" She took a swallow of beer. "Didn't see the sperm donor for almost two weeks." Dot had swivelled around on her stool, feet dangling above the rungs, and invited the woman to come on her show.

"Dot!" always started with a light, mildly humorous item, before moving on to the serious stuff. This segment featured squabbling neighbours, family spats, and the increasingly popular "forgive a stranger" bits like a paraplegic forgiving a woman who always parked in a handicapped spot at Costco to get closer to the entrance.

A week later, the pregnant woman, now in a tidy blouse with a Peter Pan collar, much to Dot's disappointment, sat in the green room admiring the furniture. "Everything in here matches," she said, "even the pictures." Beside her sat her reluctant boyfriend who was wearing a cow's skull bolo tie and grumbling aloud that he wasn't going to say sorry, *especially* as he *wasn't*. "You don't have to say anything," a chase producer assured him. Dot popped in to wave hello to all the guests (who included a six-year-old boy who had brought a peanut-butter sandwich to school, causing a classmate to have a fatal anaphylactic reaction). Dot said to the boyfriend, "This isn't the *apology* show. This is the forgiveness show." She squatted down in her high-voltage red cashmere suit that felt so good against her skin she almost had to take a cold shower to keep from screaming with joy and rested her fingertips on his knees. "You just have to sit there while she forgives you for being a big oaf."

"Crying is optional," the chase producer said.

"If you cry," his girlfriend told him, "we get an extra mug."

Back in her office, Dot's hand still tingles from the cameraman's touch. On the monitor directly in front of her that ad is running again. The couple spin around in slow motion in each other's arms. The showroom staff beam and applaud. She decides she will ban the Saturn commercial from airing on "Dot!" She'll say it reminds her of that terrible night the mad swami and his preppy girlfriend, that teen terrorist, commandeered the car with the babyseat in the back, and, yes, though it's true she's forgiven them, the image is seared into her brain. Flashbacks, you understand. Her daughter. The empty babyseat. Doesn't take a rocket scientist. Need I say another word. Covers her face with one hand, flaps her would-be consolers away with the other.

She glimpses herself practising this in the mirror hanging on the back of her office door and can't help but think she looks rather fetching.

The first thing Dorothy noticed as she was guided to her seat at the trial, a box of three-ply Kleenex under one arm and the strange buzzing in her head that had started the night of the explosion and still hadn't gone away, was that it seemed a lot like church, what with all the people filing into the pews and something that looked like an altar up front. There was even a guy whose job it was to carry the Bible around, like some kind of altar boy, although he mostly kept it tucked under his arm like a newspaper. The second thing she noticed was that people were looking at her, not through her, and not like she was some kind of animal in the zoo (*Holy smoke, lookit the size of that thing! Get the camera!*), but right at her with something that looked alarmingly like sympathy.

That was enough to start her sniffling, but what really set Dorothy off was the bright-blonde teen terrorist with the clear skin and the raccoon eyes. So assured. So smart. So ladylike. She sat with her hands in her lap, didn't *fiddle*, and even when those big-shot lawyers grilled her, she never once hung her head, hair covering her eyes. One by one, witnesses were trotted out to attest to her character. A crumbling piano teacher, all hoity-toity with her tea-biscuit accent, shaking as hard as the bug-eyed dog under her arm; a nurse pushing some really screwed-up kid in a wheelchair who started waving his balled-up fists over his head and laughing in great honks as soon as he saw the girl. Well, don't have a conniption, Dorothy couldn't help thinking, although she knew you'd have to be a numb-bum not to be impressed by this cheerleading section. But the whole time the blonde girl's mother just sat at the back of the courtroom and never looked directly at her daughter. Dorothy found this so tragic she started crying and once she got started she just couldn't stop.

She cried because she'd had a daughter like Gloria rather than this pretty little thing who was like a doll or a character right out of a movie. She could even play piano, for God's sake, and she'd won a national essay contest—an essay contest, yikes! Gloria couldn't write *Happy Birthday, Mom* on a card without making a mess. Dorothy had tried with the kid, she was sure she had, but didn't a kid have to try, too? She had even, once when Gloria was little, taken her for a pony ride in Stanley Park—three bus connections and Dorothy with all her spring allergies acting up—but the kid had started bawling and gone as stiff as a board when the attendant tried to put her on and Dorothy had had to carry her back to the bus stop under her arm like a plank. A wailing plank that she felt like just dropping into the duck pond while no one was watching. Behind them, children with hair like dandelion fluff rode the ponies around and around.

She cried because she wanted to believe that Gloria had been in the pizza place where she'd worked part-time ("pizza *parlour*," Dorothy had told Margo at work, which helped make it sound like it wasn't just a hole in the wall), trying to save a cat, because that's what the police said, that's what that growing crowd of animal activists in *Gloria!* T-shirts who gathered each day outside the provincial court building believed, and that's what Exhibit C, the charcoal calico in a plastic Ziploc bag with Gloria's blood type dried onto one of its front claws, seemed to indicate. And yet, a mother knows.

She cried because she did believe the father of the almost dead man lying in St. Paul's burn unit—the mastermind who had been driving the getaway car—when he put his hand on the Bible and swore that his son was a pacifist, a follower of Gandhi. One side of his mouth sagged as if he'd had a stroke and he had dusty brown skin, but Dorothy figured he was all right. The type of guy she wouldn't mind for a neighbour. He looked kind. Which got her thinking of that movie with Marlon Brando and wishing she was the sort of woman who could stand up and say—with a dreamy Southern accent like she'd just got out of bed and was wearing a wrinkled but 100 percent silk slip—*I always rely on the kindness of strangers.*

Dorothy cried through the remaining forty days of the trial, didn't eat, didn't sleep, just kept on crying, weeping so profusely the flesh began to melt away from her bones. And when it came time for her victim-impact statement she finally noticed none of her clothes even remotely fit any more and she had to go to Value Village to get a new outfit. She came out of the change room in a size eight, an acrylic knit (*a clingy knit!*), and couldn't keep from smiling a watery little smile, even though the hem was unravelling and she had to roll up the sleeves

so that a spot of fabric near one elbow that had melted—
fused together and turned brown—wouldn't show.

Just before Dorothy took the stand, a blast victim
who now had a plastic disc in his skull told the court
how lucky he was. The man had been the janitor at the
laundromat next to Tony's that had also been destroyed.
He'd gone outside for a smoke and saw someone he
would later identify as the teen terrorist ("she appeared
out of nowhere") throw something through the back
window of Tony's. He remembered lighting another cigarette and thinking the girl had nice hair ("it sort of
floated out behind her as she ran down the alley") and
that's the last thing he remembered.

"I was going to quit, my girlfriend really wanted me
to quit. But now I've realized it's my karma to smoke," he
said, smoothing his shaved scalp with yellowed fingers.
Then he glazed over and the only sound in the courtroom for almost a full minute was Dorothy's crying,
which had by now become a kind of white noise. "Sorry,"
the guy said when he came to, "that's just the inner-ear
damage. I wish I had a metal plate." He paused and smiled.
"Can't pick up too many stations with this plastic one." A
couple of people laughed. "Kid*ding*." More people laughed.
"What I really want to say is that I'm not bitter. They
did something they believed in and now they're paying
the price."

Dorothy thought the guy was nuts not to be pissed
off—and what with part of his brain lopped off, maybe he
was—but a murmur of admiration rippled through the
spectators and some of the regulars even began to clap.

So when Dorothy stood in front of them, tears streaming down her face, and said that she, too, wasn't bitter, the reaction was thunderous. It was true, as some of the news reports had put it, that her Gloria had been killed by friendly fire, what with animal lovers killing another animal lover. "It's like shooting the puck into the net behind your own goalie, eh?" She got even more laughs than the brain-damaged guy and Dorothy realized she somehow knew, intuitively, how to play to a crowd. Then she said, because she remembered it from a movie and because it seemed the thing to say, "I just hope Gloria didn't die in vain."

Outside, the two former anarchists, who earlier had announced their decision to renounce violence to go into nursing so they could help improve living conditions on northern native reserves, dropped to their knees in front of Dorothy on the courthouse steps following their conditional discharge and begged forgiveness. And Dorothy, in a gesture that would become her trademark, opened her arms wide and hugged them, clutching them against her so that she could feel their hearts racing, smell their smoky, nacho breath, the faint animal odour from their nervous, bushy armpits. She couldn't remember the last time she had willingly held another body against her own, the last time she'd hugged her own daughter. She almost couldn't let them go.

The crowd of people gathered outside spontaneously burst into applause. Then dozens of whooping spectators surged up the steps and hoisted, first Dorothy, then the man with the plastic disc in his head, into the air like the bride and groom at a Jewish wedding. Soon the two former anarchists were bobbing about on the shoulders of the crowd as well. And although Dorothy was worried her underwear and the network of exploded veins in her thighs would show, she had to admit that the view from on top was really something.

During the following days and weeks, the media tried to make sense of this unexpected outburst of goodwill in the wake of such tragedy. "Dawn of the Nice Age," more than one headline read. An evolutionary biologist from Simon Fraser University weighed in with a piece in *Maclean's* on the possibility of the forgiveness gene. "The Journal" had on a psychology professor from York who told Barbara Frum, "The victim forgiving the victimizer —not in a mytho-religious sense, but in its pure, undiluted form—is a terrifically empowering force, equal to, or even surpassing, vengeance. I've worked it out mathematically." He shoved a sheet of paper at her which she examined politely, nodding her head. And "Morningside" featured a panel, including Eugene Whelan, who argued, congenially, that this kind of forgiveness was a uniquely Canadian phenomenon.

But Dorothy, who had watched the coverage that first night after squeezing several drops of Visine into each of her eyes and squirming against the pinchy feeling as it dripped into the back of her nose, recognized it for what it was. Entertainment.

She hadn't sat glued to the couch watching all those years of daytime TV for nothing.

That old teacher of Gloria's is right, she has to do something really special to mark the tenth anniversary of her daughter's death, Dot thinks, reaching under her desk to massage her toes. No matter how exquisitely crafted her shoes are, her feet always hurt. A phantom pain, her therapist has told her, as if they're still carrying her now phantom weight.

The parks board had finally approved that statue for Stanley Park that the SPCA & Friends had lobbied for. The bombing site was now a free walk-in veterinary clinic mostly used by squeegee kids for their inevitable dogs, although Dot thinks the vets should delouse the kids, with their gnarled hair and wasp's-nest clothing, while they're at it. (Once, a few months after the firebombing, Dot, then still Dorothy, had stood at the edge of the small crater and stared hard into it, but it was like looking into space when you didn't have a bloody clue what you were searching for. In a movie she would've found something, a locket? a bracelet? a watch stopped at zero hour? that whispered of lost possibilities. Or, at the very least, a bloodied hand would've shot up out of the earth and tried to claw the heart out of her chest. But nothing.) Then there's the group that's written to the pope about beatifying Gloria, which Dot understands is like being an apprentice saint, sort of like an assistant electrician, or the first runner-up in the Miss Universe pageant. *And should the winner not be able to fulfill her term...* She likes the sound of it, beatifying, like sending Gloria off to some swanky spa for a complete makeover. *Dear John Paul Two, while you're at it, could you do something about her complexion if it's not too much trouble?*

The whole Vatican thing is just peeing up a wind tunnel, as her mother would've said. But there's no denying Gloria has a following. That young singer, the one from the Maritimes who now lives in Vancouver and has a platinum record and some kind of girl-power concert tour, has even written a song about her: "Feline Spirit"— an atonal little number, in Dot's opinion, but popular with teenaged girls who don't shave their legs and wear thick woollen toques even in warm weather.

Dot has no idea what she can possibly do on the show that would pack the right degree of emotional wallop, short of having Gloria rise from the dead and forgive her killer, live-to-tape right there in front of a studio audience. Her thumb, which is firmly circling her left instep, slowly comes to a stop. A cool mist, a mountain-fresh blast of an idea, wafts through her brain, tightening the skin over her skull as it grows. The idea hurls Dot, still in her stocking feet, down the hall towards the producer's office.

"The little kid last week with the sandwich was good, but I can't believe he didn't cry when the dead boy's mother read that poem by her son. *I* almost cried," Dot's producer is telling someone over the phone. She motions for Dot to have a seat, then makes a little yap yap yap motion with her thumb and fingers and rolls her eyes. "Of course it wasn't a great poem. He was what? Five? Can you hold a sec?" She glances up to see Dot still standing. "No, actually I gotta go."

She looks at Dot intensely. "Dot, honestly, what do you think of my bangs? Too long? Too short?" She palms her hair flat against her forehead so Dot can see the full effect and then sighs. "Who am I kidding? I'm too old for that Bettie Page shtick, unless I want to go for the aging-dominatrix look." She'd been manic like this lately. Dot figured it was menopause, something Dot herself was trying to stave off with a pre-emptive strike—a full-frontal estrogen assault. She'd mainline estrogen until all her veins collapsed if it would help. She'd inject it under her toenails the way models did with heroin to avoid track marks.

The producer loves the idea. She even claps her hands together like a delighted child. Dot will forgive her daughter's killer, will envelop her in her now-famous-coast-to-coast embrace, with Gloria looking down on them from enormous screens. Multiple beatific Glorias. Of course, Dot has forgiven the teen terrorist, forgiven them all, as she's often said on the show, but never in person, never in the flesh. The producer tells Dot she can already feel the ratings swell and soar, shooting right up through the stratosphere. Kleenex will be a sponsor. And just think of the cat food ads they'll sell. *Meow meow meow!* She playfully rakes the air with invisible claws. Then she shakes her head. "But no one's seen her for what? Almost eight years. Since she got out of juvie for good behaviour. She's disappeared into thin air. The news people can't even find her."

"No one disappears into thin air," Dot says.

She pauses in the producer's doorway. "Too short," she says. "Your bangs are too short. They make you look surprised all the time."

Her assistant is holding out the phone as Dot walks back into her office. "Our Lady of Sorrows. Guest sermon. The twenty-fifth." The girl was always breathless, her eyes red-rimmed under black plastic cat's-eye glasses with mica glittering across the top. At least once a week, Dot has to send her home in a cab when she looks in danger of short-circuiting. Dot takes the receiver with a secret sigh. The Catholics were becoming so demanding and they didn't even pay as well as the Evangelicals, or sing as good either. "Yup, yup," Dot says to the person at the other end of the phone, "okay, but you do realize I'm—" she puts her hand over the receiver and turns to her assistant. "Ecumenical," the girl stage-whispers. "Ecumenical," Dot says into the telephone, relieved that she hadn't said, "economical" by mistake.

"The rain in Spain falls mainly on the plain," Dot trills as she hangs up.

On cue, her assistant asks in a half-hearted sing-song, pointing the tip of her pen at Dot. "And where's that blasted plain?" This is why Dot pays her the big bucks.

"In Spain! In Spain!" Dot raises her arms. "In Spaaaain!"

The fact that she'd practised that with marbles in her mouth was something nobody needed to know.

If there was a moment when her world irrevocably turned from black and white to colour, if Dorothy could actually pinpoint it, she would have to say it was in the Mondi boutique on level three of the Holt Renfrew off Granville Street, while she was trying on a dress to wear for the premiere of "Dot!" on BCTV (before "Dot!" was

syndicated and really took off) following the unprece-
dented success of her weekly Rogers Cable show. She'd
never even dared enter the store before (T-shirts were
three hundred bucks. *T-shirts!* That'd be for people with
more money than brains.), and gliding up the escalator
she felt like she was in Buckingham Palace. She thought
maybe she should've bought a ticket just to be allowed a
look-see. At the bottom of the escalator, an elegant girl
with a black velvet bow in her hair had misted her wrist
with perfume and as Dorothy rose above the glittering
concourse the scent swirled around her like the sweet,
alien breath of some fairy godmother.

The saleswoman, who looked like she rode horses
sidesaddle in her spare time, said, "I must say, that looks
incredible with your skin tone."

Dorothy twirled in front of the three-way mirror,
thinking the woman was just blowing sunshine up
her arse. But she had to admit she couldn't recognize
herself.

"Do you have this in any other colour?" she asked.

"Zabaglione, persimmon, tamarind, and quince."

There were colours in the world she hadn't even
known existed and this woman—who, when you stopped
to think about it, was just a clerk, right?—was reeling
them off casually like she was reciting the alphabet.

Gloria, Dorothy whispered, *I don't think we're in Kansas
anymore*. Shocking herself that she was talking to her
dead daughter. But then again, maybe not that much had
changed. Gloria didn't answer.

The "Dot!" team is caught up in a debate over a promo for the *Gloria!* special which uses a bit of footage from the bombing of Hiroshima. ("My grandparents were put in an internment camp right here in B.C.," says the associate producer, who Dot always assumed was Scottish. "It's a death-to-life thing," the editor tells her in that patient tone used with four-year-olds while pulling on their socks, "a visual metaphor.") One of the chase producers, who has spent weeks with the phone glued to her ear tracking down the former teen terrorist, appears in the doorway of the editing suite, her mouth opening and closing silently as if she was underwater gumming fish flakes. Finally, she blurts, "I found her!" The editor pauses the tape and everyone looks up.

The chase producer is quiet for a moment, kneading her abdomen as if she has cramps. On the video monitor a puffy mushroom cloud is three-quarters through its transformation into the word *Dot!* "She says she doesn't want to be forgiven."

She doesn't want to be forgiven? All the women blink in the half-light—they're all women here in this forgiveness business (surprise!)—and take it up as a mantra. *She doesn't want to be forgiven.* Then, one by one, they look towards Dot, faces pinched into question marks, even the executive producer, a wisecracking TV veteran who got her start as the voice of a famously androgynous puppet on a long-running kids show.

Is this what they call being up against the wall? These women, with all their B.A.s and M.A.s and phi beta cum laudy laudies have little imagination and even less faith,

Dot thinks. They've never had to really work at anything. They've never had their stomachs stapled, their rent cheques bounce, daughters who left used Kotexes balled up under their beds for the cat to drag out and bat around the apartment, never had to handle bloody, leaking packages of meat for customers who would sooner spit at her than say, *Gee thanks*, never had people come up to them at bus stops, complete strangers, and tell them that if they just tried a little harder, used that old willpower, laid off the Timbits, they could get, well, you know—

"I'll forgive her skanky little butt whether she likes it or not," Dot tells them, the long-dead Dorothy creeping into her voice. She starts giving orders, telling them to book the teen terrorist's mother, the guy with the plate in his head, the man whose pacifist son burned to eventual death, the chorus line of *Cats*, now playing at the Ford Centre, that girl-power singer, who could perform her Gloria anthem. Maybe even one of those Three Tenors—Pavarotti, or Domingo, or that other guy—anyone could be had for a price. Why not?! *My dad's got a barn, let's put on a show!*

The marrow in Dot's bones thickens and she can feel the blood moving through her body, slamming in and out of the sluice gates of her heart. She's clamped onto that circus wire with an iron jaw and she'll keep hanging on, even if her teeth splinter and her gums shred, as high above her on a platform a handsome man in purple tights twirls her in tight circles until she's nothing but a blur of airborne colour, and the crowd, though they've seen her do this a hundred times before, holds its breath.

The trick is to keep your tongue away from the roof of your mouth.

III. HER MOTHER

You try with a child. You even strain their shit, pushing it through a sieve with the back of a spoon to make sure they've passed the marble they've swallowed in a fit of pique. You dress them up as gypsy fortunetellers, lady-bugs, and mermaids, sewing each sequin on by hand in the dampish 4 A.M. basement, so as not to spoil the surprise, so as to finish the damn thing in all its glory before making yet another Sanka and leaving for work, bags billowing under your eyes, nerves jitterbugging, phantom sequins scratching the back of your throat. But Lucy, as an actuary, as a woman whose profession it is to calculate risk, usually knows how to figure out the balance of probability in favour of something happening. The one risk she hadn't calculated, though, were the odds that a child could strip-mine your heart.

But what about the odds that in April 1965 a child will be born who is perfect, glistening like a rainbow trout, but with ears and fingers and toes and a potential for greatness that makes her father swell with a pride so large he can barely squeeze his hard hat back on after leaving the hospital called Holy Something, and that exactly four years to the day this child is born, this same father will tragically (later perversely recalled by the child as intentionally)

stall his 1967 Valiant on the railway tracks he and his wife
and the shiny child live on the right side of (thank God),
and that in the aftermath of this indescribable mess, this
psychic black hole, the mother decides that the life of
the second child, another daughter (she *feels* it), the one
no one yet knows of, will not be worth a copper penny,
so that she proceeds accordingly but is never again without the sensation that a small animal is chewing a hole
through her throat from the inside out?

Or the odds that a mother wouldn't notice that a child
never sleeps, or notices but convinces herself that the
girl is sleeping, eyes open wide, skin glowing in the
moonlight like phosphorescence?

Or the odds that when your teenage daughter jangles
around the kitchen, trying to make herself understood,
trying to tell you that she has no idea what it means to
be happy, while you're up to your elbows in suds, hands
crabbing for cutlery in the sink, you'll have the right
answer to the question, "Why can't I be up all the time?
Why can't I be *on*?"

Or the odds that when the phone call comes you will
keep thinking, despite the facts at hand, the evidence, as
it's called, that it's your own daughter who's dead, because
then you can let yourself drop into the soft pocket of
grief, whereas the truth has its undefinable ragged edges,
its welcome-to-the-funhouse tilt that keeps you so off
balance it's hard to know if you're coming or going—or

gone? So off balance in fact that when the time comes you can't tell the requisite stories, the ones everyone expects to hear, the ones that begin: *She wouldn't hurt a fly...*

Then there are the odds, and these are far from slim, of dreaming night after night of a luminous girl with wide eyes, nerves wavering like tentacles above her head, then waking and always wondering, *Which daughter is this?*

And waiting to be struck by lightning.

IV. HER VICTIM

What is there to say? There is the shade of this arbutus tree near where my ashes are scattered. Someone told my mother it would give my soul peace and she said, yeah okay, whatever. Its bark, the way it hangs down in spots all shaggy, brutish and short, resembles a haircut I once had. It hung down over my eyes, hiding a moonscape of pimples across my expansive, domed forehead. I could see everyone through my shag, but they couldn't see me. I was the one who sat beside you sucking on my hair, shredding paper, my fingers spiky with hangnails, carving misspelled words into the skin of my arms till I bled.

In life I could barely string a sentence together. In death I am eloquent. Now I write poetry in my head. Not just free verse, but everything from Spenserian sonnets and madrigals to neo-formalist villanelles. And you should see me on the uneven bars. Those anorexic little Romanian girls better watch *out.*

I tell you. Death is *great*. Even my acne has cleared up.
Death, the ultimate Ten-O-Six pad.

When the reporters descended on Britannia High like
members of the Canadian Airborne, everyone panicked.
There were all those microphones and video cameras and
pens poised over steno pads waiting to get the quotes that
would get the shock waves going, start the tears flowing.
I mean, what could they *say*? That I laughed like a hyena,
that I always dropped the ball, that my breath knocked
them flat on their backs, that I seemed forever to be *dripping* from one orifice or another? (I had some hobbies
most normals wouldn't approve of. I loved the taste and
smell of myself, my own salty spew, my own jam, my personal cheese, the ongoing mystery of *me*.) So they had no
choice, they made stuff up.

A personality emerged, a social history, an innocent
heart. Someone remembered that I sang, well, hummed
under my breath, once maybe, perhaps for a second,
could have been clearing my throat, could have been gagging on a potato chip, but soon I was an aspiring opera
singer, a soprano who could break your heart, a Mimi, a
Carmen, that guys could die of love for. It took a few days,
maybe even a whole week, but old boyfriends finally
began to appear, materializing out of nowhere like the
ghost of Christmas yet to come. I was shy, a virgin even,
but it seemed I had a gift for breaking hearts. One guy,
his beautiful pouty mouth all chapped and cracked from
a long summer of island tree planting, his tanned knees
bursting from his jeans, appeared on "MuchWest" and
told Terry David Mulligan my favourite song was some-

thing called "Rise Up!"—which I'd never even heard of. And then, his eyes filled with what looked to be real tears while Terry David Mulligan stared intently at his own ankle, his argyle-clad ankle crossed over his knee, as if to make sure it was still there. His ankle bone connected to his leg bone, his leg bone connected to his thigh bone, and so on and so on, marvelling at how connected he felt at that very moment to other people and to his very own self. Either that, or he was sadly unequipped to deal with watching another guy cry.

People kept confusing our pictures, me and that preppy urban guerilla girl. They thought the sunny, smiling teen was the victim, while the sullen one with the bad skin who wouldn't look at the camera was the junior terrorist. Even the newspapers did it, switching the cutlines as if trying to fix a case of mistaken identities.

Two little girls from next door, the ones who used to call me Cousin It, tips of their tongues blue from licking Kool-Aid powder darting in and out gecko-style in my general direction, begged their mothers to take them to see where it had happened. They stood there at the edge of that small apocalypse, that sorry little pit, and threw their favourite stuffed animals in. By the following morning, the hole that'd once been Tony's wholly mediocre Pizza & Donair was brimming with plush toys like a carnival stall. Sure, a few of the kids were encouraged to be unselfish by their parents, but if their reach didn't exceed their grasp, what's a parent for? (Carnies of the soul, forever crying out, "Step right up!" while all you want to do is pull the covers up over your head and sleep, breathing in your own musty fug, gathering your strength like a dust bunny gathers fur.) And you never did know whose Kirsten or Jason just might appear on page three the next day, or on the six o'clock news that very night.

Oh, those heady days of Hallmark moments, kaleidoscope of love. And small miracles. The dirt from the pit made a deep-cleansing, cruelty-free facial mask and cured anxiety. Crocuses pushed their crowns through the ground five months early while cardboard jack-o'-lanterns grinned from store windows. The lights along Venables turned green in succession at *exactly the right moment*. Drivers became believers.

All this fuss because of a cat. A cat by the name of Elliott who didn't really belong to anyone, but who Tony and his half-wit brother Enzo let gnaw on leathery curls of pepperoni or donair meat shavings that fell to the floor in return for tussling with mice and the occasional Norwegian rat. A mercenary who, when you really think about it, had a better life than mine, who had no greater measure than his own nature to contend with, and whose tail I'd stepped on more than once just to let him know that I knew that he knew this too.

What, then, was I doing there that time of night? My head in the pizza oven in some weak approximation of Sylvia Plath, *The Bell Jar* ringing through my head. I had to sit on a stool and stick my head in up to the shoulder. It wasn't until my skin started to bubble up and I realized I wasn't dead that I knew what a true screw-up I was right to the end. It wasn't even a gas oven. (*It wasn't even a gas oven.* This repeats over and over in my mind like a punch-line that takes too long to get.) I was screaming and pressing ice cubes from the pop machine to my ear when the explosion came.

They say it only took a second, but when you're in the middle of the vortex time really does stand still. The pressed meat unfurled from the spit, almost elegantly, with a kind of balletic grace. Bottles of hot sauce heaved, then spewed upwards like small volcanoes. A broom waltzed across the floor. Elliott the cat spun end over end overhead as if tumbling around in an industrial-strength dryer. And for the first and last time while I was alive, I thought about the kid. Before that I couldn't imagine it as anything much more than a jelly bean once the candy-coating had been sucked off. This translucent kidney bean of snarled DNA wedged somewhere above my coiled intestines, this thing that could destroy me. As Tony's burst into flame, I thought... maybe the kid'd be cute, smell of oven-fresh buns, as they say. Maybe I once did, too. Maybe there was a moment when my mother bent to sniff the top of my head and tears filled the corners of her mouth (*sharply*, as they say) because she caught a whiff of possibility from the milky sweat of my scalp.

Maybe Enzo would've liked his kid, maybe it would've had a chance. It was Enzo that was supposed to find me when he opened up in the morning, his dopey Sly Stallone eyes opening wide, lids pressing up against gravity, his little mouth saying, "Noooooooo!" as his whole crummy world collapsed all around him.

When your dead love hits your eye like a big pizza pie, that's amore!

They always realize too late that they actually loved you.

My tongue, that fat slug that snapped back like a window blind to block my throat every time I slid from my desk and rattled around on the floor—voodoo curse, epilepsy—scaring the shit out of everyone while the teacher struggled with a ruler to separate my tongue from my throat, scraping the skin off the roof of my mouth, skin that later hung like tattered cobwebs and that I loved to worry with the tip of that same tongue until I couldn't stand it any more and tore the strips off and ate them, that same tongue is now quicksilver— skywriting, bronc-busting, slipping into your bed, tasting everything first, the small blue spot you see on your television screen before the picture snuffs out completely.

Being martyred is a class act.

I'm supposed to be wise now, like a genie or something. Grant you three wishes, that kind of thing.

Tell you what. When that statue of me and Elliott goes up in Stanley Park near Lumberman's Arch, you're welcome to come and kiss my shiny bronze ass. Then see what happens.

V. HER APPEARANCE

A P.A. is attaching Dot's wireless mike backstage when Lucy is brought over to meet her. Dot is surprised to find

Lucy so plain, she'd remembered the teen terrorist's mother as a handsome woman from the trial. And all that grey, in this day and age when, if you can't afford to go to a salon, all you need is five minutes, a bathroom sink, and a pair of rubber gloves.

Lucy is surprised as well. Not a day has gone by over the past ten years when she hasn't found her hands shaking so uncontrollably she could barely punch a few numbers accurately into a calculator without the aid of beta blockers. But today, of all days, not a tremor. She could pluck a pin off a slippery linoleum floor, conduct brain surgery, skin a flea.

The former teen terrorist is surprised to find herself there at all, sitting high up in the packed temporary bleachers near the back of the studio with the overflow audience, sunglasses on, a baseball cap pulled low over her forehead, watching the still empty set. The ads said her mother would be there. The ads said *she* would be there, even after she'd said no, absolutely not, piss off. She smiles to think what fools these TV people are to assume she'd show up after all and parade, contrite, in front of their cameras. Did they think they'd just flush her out like some kind of grouse?

Dot walks onto the set. The show's theme music starts up and mushroom clouds explode across the expanse of multiple video screens spelling out *Dot!*

The pancake makeup on Lucy's face feels like a mask. She blinks her eyes and wiggles her lips just to make sure she's still real.

The two women on either side of the former teen

terrorist, wearing ski jackets and dress pants, hoot and holler and stamp their feet. She can feel the bleacher rumbling under the soles of her shoes.

The producer, her bangs longer now, fluffier, sings into Dot's earpiece from the control booth, *Meow meow meow!*

A face appears on the video screens. Multiple beatific Glorias. The twice-platinum girl-power singer, hair held off her face with tiny, plastic duck barrettes, sings "Feline Spirit." A cluster of sad-mouthed young women in the audience, dressed in long India-cotton skirts with Guatemalan scarves looped around their necks entwine fingers and sway back and forth, singing along to the chorus.

Dot looks up at the sunny, smiling blonde teen on the video screens and the lump in her throat feels unaccountably real.

Lucy, watching on a monitor off-set, shuts her lids over her burning eyes.

The former teen terrorist watches with disbelief from behind her dark glasses as she looks into her own face, her own high school photo, projected on the screens above the set, with the name *Gloria* scrawled underneath.

Dot hugs Lucy. The audience applauds. *Like Lennon's auntie hugging Chapman's mom*, a newspaper reporter stage-whispers to another, then writes this down. Dot throws to a commercial for Purina Cat Chow. The audience, prompted by an androgynous teenager wearing a Cat in the Hat T-shirt, sings the chorus from "Feline Spirit" again. Waiting in the green room, the man with the plastic disc in his head thinks he's finally tuned in to the right station.

The audience is hushed as Dot announces the former teen terrorist. They want to see her forgiven—and they don't. They don't *know*. A young woman with poor posture, head hanging, dark hair covering her eyes, makes her way on to the set. She drops to her knees in front of Dot and Lucy and the man with the disc in his head. Dot urges her to stand up and then wraps her arms around her in a full embrace. The audience goes wild, whistling, clapping, stamping their feet like a drum roll. From her place high in the bleachers, the former teen terrorist numbly watches as this dumpy actress who looks nothing like her is forgiven. The producer watches the ratings visibly swell and soar.

Lucy daydreams of a child, born perfect, glistening like a rainbow trout.

While still hugging the penitent to her breast, Dot closes her eyes and lets the applause wash over her. Purging her.

But if anyone dared ask, say a someone at a book signing while she held her Waterford mid *Dot!*, or a curious seamstress with a mouth full of pins kneeling at her feet while she was trying on an outfit at Boboli for the annual Black & White fundraiser at the Vancouver Art Gallery, or, yes, another mother right here in the studio, if that someone, looked right into her eyes and asked *the question*, the only real question, the Frank Capra question: If you could have your daughter alive again and everything went back to the way it was before... the mother of the victim, this Dorothy who's now a Dot, who's five sizes smaller and who feels so *alive*, alive in her electrifying sadness and her Italian leather shoes, would open her mouth to answer, but instead of words something else would come out. A small bat, blind under the studio lights, swooping in drunken helixes back and forth overhead while everyone screams and runs for cover, their fingers splayed wide over their hair.

acknowledgements

I am indebted to the now sadly defunct Explorations Program of the Canada Council and Richard Holden, wherever he may be; *The New Quarterly* for being first; and Keith Maillard and Linda Svendsen. Big thanks to Caroline Adderson, Roxanna Bikadoroff, Peter Eastwood, Anne Fleming, Jillian Hull, Murray (phone buddy) Logan, Shelley MacDonald, Maureen Medved, Shannon Stewart, and Shelley Youngblut for expansive hearts and minds. Very special thanks to Patty Jones for her particular brand of cunning, and to Ginny Ratsoy, Jim Satterthwaite, Allison Sullings, Dianna Symonds, and my mother, Irma Varadi, for never doubting writers matter; and, above all, to my editor, Patrick Crean, for Perkinsesque patience, enthusiasm, wisdom & cheer beyond the call of duty. And, of course, of course, there is John Dippong, my alpha and omega.